The Rose of the Ribble Valley

To Joan
Best wishes
Graham Dixon

PlaneTree

The Rose of the Ribble Valley

by

Graham Dixon

Published 2002
ISBN 1-84294-100-3

Published by PlaneTree

Old Station Offices,
Llanidloes,
Powys SY18 6EB
United Kingdom

Manufactured in the United Kingdom

To Bernadette.

The finest singer I know:

And the best wife in the world.

Acknowledgements.

Thanks to Harold Dearden and his son Paul. Harold read my final draft; giving me another musician's valued opinion on the story and Paul painstakingly went through it checking the grammar etc.

Thanks to Ross Dixon for sorting out the cover.

Also thanks to the members of The Preston Writers Guild for their advice, encouragement and friendship.

About the author.

Graham Dixon lives in The Lancashire Village of Gregson Lane, which lies about 4 miles south of the 'new' City of Preston.

Although, by profession, Graham is a Quality Controller in the Aerospace industry, his first love has always been 'Popular Folk Music'. He spends much of his time either entertaining people whilst playing with his band 'Trouble at' Mill' or as Organiser of the popular Gregson Lane Folk Club that has been meeting, in the village, bi-weekly for over 15 years.

The Rose of The Ribble Valley is Graham's first novel, however he has appeared in print many times. His concert and folk club reviews have often graced the pages of local folk music publications and he has also had an article published in Garden News.

Graham publishes a Lancashire Dialect Dictionary on the Internet at www.troubleatmill.btinternet.co.uk the website is also visited regularly by hundreds of people who want to know 'What's on' in the folk clubs of Northwest England.

Graham has been married to fellow Trouble at' Mill member - Bernadette for 23 years. They have two sons Ross & Ryan who are both musicians.

Grahams motto, which appears on the publicity posters and tickets for any event that he is involved with, is: -

KEEP MUSIC LIVE.

Foreword.

The Rose Of The Ribble Valley is set in the area south of the River Ribble - between Preston and Clitheroe.

There are several popular Folk Music Venues in the Area; Gregson Lane Folk Club at Hoghton and Blackburn Folk Club plus 'singers nights that take place regularly in Walton le Dale, Osbaldeston, Clitheroe, Longridge and Pleasington.

All the venues are frequented by bands like 'Elderflower Punch', duos similar to Pushing Forté, guitarists like 'Woody' and folksingers not unlike Brian Clayton and Mary Jones. However the artistes in the story are all fictional characters and any resemblance to actual people is purely coincidental (though often unavoidable).

The pubs and clubs herein are all fictional too although similarities to actual venues may be evident.

If you are in this part of the country and would like to sample some Folk Music in Lancashire then log on to the Internet at www.troubleatmill.com and find details therein.

As for the dreaded PEL (Public Entertainment License) the legislation that is responsible for the ridiculous (now widely known as) 'Two In A Bar Rule' have a look at the appendix at the back of the book which contains a transcript of an interview from The Mike Harding Show, on Radio 2. Mike kindly gave me his permission to use it.

There is also a song by Roger Gall. Who, at the time of writing is a passionate campaigner for the abolition of the P.E.L. Roger kindly gave me permission to use it.

Finally possession and consumption of psilicybin for 'Recreational purposes' are offences under the Misuse of Drugs Act. 1970.

THE ROSE OF THE RIBBLE VALLEY.

Prologue

Geoff.

"Mush a ring a ma doo a ma day - whack fol my daddio whack fol my daddio there's whiskey in the jar - HEY."

Geoff always finished off with Kilgarry Mountain. The loud shout of "HEY," at the end of the song, which was enhanced by the sudden addition of a pulsating 'foot-switched' echo, was like drawing a final line under the evening's performance.

Although not exactly rapturous, the applause was, in the main, warm and well meant. It was punctuated with whistles and shouts of "MORE." However, Geoff had been in the business long enough to know that these insincere calls for an encore were not from his regular followers but from the 'noisy drunken bastards' at the bar, who had not listened to one song all night and were now shouting in the forlorn hope that maybe another chorus would encourage Brian, the landlord, to take the towels off the beer pumps and continue to serve after hours. No chance!

Geoff stepped back from the microphone and unplugged the fluorescent pink lead from his Martin Dreadnought guitar, unhitched the strap and placed the instrument safely into its fur-lined flight case. Protect the guitar, that's the most important bit of kit, everything else was replaceable and could be packed away later after a well-deserved wind down over a couple of pints of Brian's award winning 'real ale'.

Out from behind the bar, Brian stepped over to microphone and beckoned to Geoff as if to say, "Is it still switched on?"

Geoff nodded.

"LADIES AND GENTLEMEN, CAN WE HAVE YOUR GLASSES EMPTIED PLEASE!" boomed the landlord's voice, with an air of confidence that demonstrated his well-practised microphone technique.

Geoff looked across at Wayne, the bass player, and shrugged his shoulders, knowing that his fellow musician was also thinking that it would make a pleasant change if the landlord, while he had the microphone, would take the opportunity to actually thank the band for their efforts. Not Brian! After playing the folk cubs and pubs himself, for more years than he cared to remember, Brian had little time for the niceties of the 'local' live music scene. He had now discovered that the only way to make any money out of it was to get on the business side of the bar and rake in the profits from the drinks.

Now that the towels were up, Brian's sole purpose in life was to get the place empty. He could then count, not only the money in the till but also the money in the drawer under the bar, which any sober, observant customer would have noticed was used for Brian's 'Special Offers' such as: cling film wrapped sandwiches and baguettes; cigarettes brought in on the back of lorries from the continent and the proceeds of 'The Doubles Bar', which offered large measures of spirits, all of which where supermarkets' 'own' brands, at a discount price.

Wayne made an obscene gesture with his right hand behind Brian's back.

Grinning as he coiled the guitar lead around his arm, Geoff stepped across and quietly commented as he looked up at Wayne's smiling face. "He may be a wanker but he pays the money."

"Bastard must have taken well over five hundred quid the place was bloody well heaving," said Wayne as he lifted one of the heavy cabinets containing a 15-inch loudspeaker from the top of the speaker stand. "And I'm getting too bloody old for all this humping and bloody carting."

Geoff sniggered. He liked Wayne; he had played with him for over twenty years. The gentle giant was a musical genius and a boon to any band, whatever their style. After many years experience playing in jazz bands and in the orchestra pits of northern theatres, Wayne could not only play along with any group of musicians, he could actually embellish their sound with his exciting bass lines. Geoff was perfectly capable of performing solo, as was often the case, if he played folk clubs or village halls, but he liked having Wayne along on 'pub gigs' for three reasons. Mainly because Wayne's bass guitar style gave the sometimes-sombre folk songs an up beat almost 'rock and roll feel' that would appeal to the 'non folkies' in the audience. Secondly, he was very good with the PA system, both carrying it in and out and setting up the sound to get the best effect in any particular venue. Last, but not least, Wayne was handy to have around if ever any over enthusiastic 'hecklers' in the audience turned nasty and looked like becoming violent. Only last week a drunken Irishman, in a pub audience, had taken exception to a 'couple of English bastards' singing *Danny Boy*. One snarl from Wayne; directed straight at the offender, had the desired effect. Not surprising really, considering the bearded bass player's six foot four inch frame with shoulders and arms that bore testament to the years that Wayne had spent working hard as a labourer with the local council's road-works department.

Abigail sat on a stool at the corner of the bar caressing a large Jack Daniels. Although Brian had been very quick and efficient when ushering out the remaining punters, he knew the reason for Abigail being there and was prepared to allow her 'an after hours tipple' along with the two musicians. After all they were paying for the drinks and were daft enough to buy one for him, his first and only one of the night, he didn't see any point in making a habit of drinking away the profits.

Geoff had been talking to Abigail earlier in the evening and arranged to take her home. Many times, in the past, he had found comfort and affection between Abigail's sheets. The trouble with Abigail was that lots of other 'musos' found comfort between those sheets too, she was a 'text book groupie' and would never dream of going on a night out that didn't involve listening to some sort of 'live music' and going home with a real live musician.

She wore a dark blue T-shirt and emblazoned, in gold, on the front, right across her buxom chest, against the background of a musical stave, complete with treble clef, were the words: -

DO YOU WANT TO PLAY WITH ME?

She had shoulder length red hair and around her neck she wore a gold chain on which hung a chunky solid gold Fender Stratocaster electric guitar pendant. The 'western-cut' denim jeans and 'cow-girl' boots indicated that maybe her first love was country music.

"Cracking night tonight lads," said Brian, as he opened the drawer under the bar and took out a few notes. "I think I can safely say that you earned it tonight," as he handed eighty pounds over to Geoff.

"Cheers" said the singer quietly thinking to himself, that he could make sixty quid singing on his own for an hour and a half in an old folks' home, on a weekday afternoon and not even have the bother of having to take the sound system with him.

"Nearly forgot," said Brian "My accountant says I've got to start keeping records of my entertainment costs, so from now on I'll be needing a receipt."

"We'll be wanting more than eighty if were signing for it," retorted Geoff

"You know eighty is the limit Geoff. What do you think this is, a charity for washed up folk singers?"

4

"Bollocks," said Wayne "Eighty's the deal when it's cash in hand. You know, 'the black economy' and all that? You save and we save."

Brian grunted and turned to Geoff " You can always fuck off to the Shovel and play there instead and take Grizzly Adams here with you!"

Brian knew he was on a winner. The Malt Shovel was the only other pub in the area to put on live entertainment but it was a pub full of pratts and smooth flow beer and the entertainment usually consisted of some short skirted tart showing her arse and wailing away to poor quality backing tapes. No self-respecting muso would play there. Brian's pub however, The Grey Mare, was regarded as the best music venue in this part of Lancashire.

Wayne bid them goodnight.

"See you same time next week?" asked Brian.

Wayne looked at Geoff who shrugged his shoulders as if to say, "It's up to you."

"Suppose so said Wayne" reluctantly and he left carrying the remaining two microphone stands.

Geoff looked expectantly at Abigail "Well we'd better call it a night then." He patted her ample backside in an attempt to get her off the stool; it was also a subtle way of letting her know of his intentions for later. As they left Geoff smiled to himself knowing that while he was looking forward to spending the night with Abigail, that miserable bastard Brian was going to bed on his own, Brian's wife, Tina, had gone after just one night as Landlady of The Grey Mare.

He opened the boot and put his guitar inside. Abigail was in the passenger seat. The lights on the pub sign went out and threw the area into almost total darkness. As he walked round to the driver's door he heard an engine start at the other end of the car park and a pair of headlights instantly penetrated the blackness as the car drove towards them, wheels screeching. As it was nearly an hour since Brian had got rid of the last of his customers, Geoff's first thought was that he must have disturbed a couple of kids, shagging in the relative privacy of the country pub car park. The car slowed

5

as it drew near - the front offside window came down but Geoff was unable to make out who was driving, his eyes still on fire due to the dazzling effect of the cars main beam.

A voice came from the open window "HEY GEOFF! HOW COME YOU DIDN'T SING 'THE ROSE OF THE RIBBLE VALLEY' TONIGHT?"

Geoff felt all of a shiver, the hairs on his back stood on end - he hadn't sung, nor wanted to sing that song for quite some time.

Chapter 1

Some time in the 90s.

It was a strange time for live music and a difficult time for musicians. The pubs and clubs that had traditionally supported 'live' music had discovered the appeal of singers with backing tapes. Karaoke was in its infancy and had obviously inspired many a budding pop star to invest in a PA system (with lots of echo) a microphone and a cassette deck.

Even the over-priced music shops, which had been faithfully supported by generations of performing musicians, had jumped on the 'band wagon' and were now selling pre-recorded backing tracks. These could make any reasonable performer sound like he or she was singing with the support of a live band plus full orchestra and a whole choir-load of backing vocalists.

The less scrupulous entertainment agents got in on the act too, after signing up a few of these synthetic 'performers' they bombarded the pubs and clubs with literature explaining the economic advantages of using 'self contained' entertainment.

What swayed it, for most pub landlords, and for the concert secretaries and treasurers in smaller clubs, was the fact that this literature pointed out that: -

Employing solo singers using backing tapes, as opposed to 'live' musicians, alleviated the need for a Public Entertainment License, which cost hundreds of pounds each year. This new sort of entertainment that 'Guarantees a Big Sound' was covered by the normal PRS music license, needed for jukeboxes and 'piped in' music, which only costs a few quid.

These were the John Major years; 'Free Enterprise', 'Cost Cutting' and 'Makes Economic Sense' were the 'buzz phrases' of the era. How could any 'small time impresario ignore such economically sound advice?

There was a 'Knock-on' effect. Because attention had been drawn to these rules and regulations, the councils were now earmarking other pubs (usually situated out of town) that regularly presented live musical entertainment and had got away with never having a Public Entertainment License. However, reading between the lines, it appeared that the only time the councils ever forced the issue was if a third party actually complained to them.

Geoff sat in the small parlour of his end-terraced house listening to 'Father and Son.' He was an avid admirer of the music of Cat Stevens and *'Tea For The Tillerman'* was his favourite album. Whenever he listened to this particular track it always made him wonder what had finally persuaded the singer to 'give it all up' and become a devout Muslim? Surely nothing could be more fulfilling than performing one's own work in front of thousands of appreciative fans.

Geoff's diary was open on the coffee table, another gig crossed out. Earlier that morning Dougie, the landlord of the Brown Cow in Osbaldeston, had phoned to cancel that evening's gig, saying "Sorry Geoff, I've had the council on the blower, some bastard's bubbled me for not having the correct license, I daren't risk having bands on anymore."

Geoff had reassured Dougie that he didn't blame him. It was not only the Brown Cow that was getting hassled by the authorities. So far this summer, he'd had gigs at five other venues cancelled for similar reasons. He had also asked Dougie to let him know if, after the event, he received any flyers from Charlie Bagwell, who ran the Super Nova Entertainment Agency in Blackburn, advertising all his self contained acts. Dougie said that he would do and told Geoff that he would buy him a pint next time he called in.

"Maybe Cat Stevens got sick of all this legal shit too," thought Geoff. "Maybe that's why he buggered off to find Allah!"

When it came to playing, it was the applause from the audience that gave Geoff his fulfilment, not the fee. He'd be quite willing to play for beer. He was in a fortunate position and didn't depend on the money that he earned with the band. He had a day job as a fitter at the local Aerospace factory, so although it was a blow to his need to be creative, a few cancelled gigs would not cause him to starve. This, however, was not the case for the other members of 'Elderflower Punch.' So Geoff, being the organiser and self elected leader of the folk band, felt a certain amount of responsibility as far as keeping the diary full was concerned. Even though it was not his fault, he always felt guilty having to phone the other three to tell them the bad news.

He telephoned Wayne to tell him that he needn't bother packing the sound equipment into the car: the gig was off.

"Bollocks!" said the bass player "Not another one, they've cancelled the Tuesday Jazz Night down at the institute too, they've no fucking license either"

Geoff didn't even know that there was a Jazz Night at the local Weaver's Institute, let alone that Wayne played there, but it didn't surprise him, Wayne was in demand and was usually playing along with someone or other on most evenings of the week. Geoff was thankful that Wayne always put Elderflower Punch gigs first and made this fact plain to anyone else who needed his services.

"See you at the Hog's Head next Saturday then" said Wayne, "Oh, and can you and the other two buggars get there early? You know, before the punters, I want to try out a new mixer amp that I've borrowed, I'm thinking of buying it."

"Seven O clock then," Geoff replied, "And don't forget to bring the words to that Scottish song that you want to do."

Geoff dialled another number.

Chloe's Mum answered the phone "Yes she's in Geoff, I can hear her singing, just a minute, I'll give her a shout"

There was a dull thud, which was the sound of the receiver being put down, not too carefully, on the table. Geoff heard Mrs Walmsley's powerful Lancashire accented voice call out "CHLOE, GEOFF'S ON'T PHONE". Geoff smiled to himself - he squeezed the receiver to his ear and could hear the 'pat pat' of Chloe's feet as they came down the stairs accompanied by the unmistakable voice of Chloe singing *'Where have all the flowers gone?'*

This was par for the course, Chloe was always singing. She sang along with the car radio on the way to and from gigs and she sang along with the jukebox while they were sitting in the bar waiting to perform. Chloe had a wonderful singing voice; even in the noisiest venues the crowd would melt into quiet admiration when Chloe sang.

Geoff had seen her potential as a singer with the band when he had heard her sing an unaccompanied song at Pig and Whistle Folk Club, in Samlesbury, eighteen months earlier. He asked her to sing it again the week after but this time he accompanied her with an arpeggio guitar weaving a ripple lick in and out between her words. The audience warmed to it right away and Geoff knew that Chloe's vocals would give Elderflower Punch a much-needed boost. He asked her to join the band there and then.

"What about your two colleagues?" Chloe had asked, "Will they not object to a woman coming on board?"

"Just leave them to me" said Geoff "I know what's good for them!"

"Hi Geoff, everything OK" said Chloe in the most uninteresting monotone voice imaginable. That was Chloe though; a real split personality, a real mystery. There was no doubt that her wonderful voice gave her a 'magnetic' on-stage personality but back in the real world she came over as, to say the least, dull and uninteresting. She was quite attractive but always wore dark long clothes, which made her appear permanently in mourning for some long lost loved one. Maybe she was, Geoff had never asked her, but it was obvious that she was not looking for romance, as she showed no outward signs of any interest in either men or women.

"Hi Chloe, Dougie's just phoned, he's had to cancel tonight, in fact he's had to cancel everything."

"Don't tell me he's got license problems as well?"

"Yeah he reckons someone's bubbled him, I reckon it's that twat Bagwell."

"Well not to worry, I could do with a night off, I'm on a dig down near the river and the land-owner wants us finished for Wednesday, so we'll be pushing it. Looks like now I'll be able to grab a few extra hours before it goes dark tonight."

"OK see you at The Hog's Head Saturday; Wayne wants us there for seven, can you pick me up at six-thirty?"

"No problem Geoff, I'll see you on Saturday then"

He smiled to himself as he thought of another good reason for having Chloe in the band, she usually drank fruit juice and was always willing to drive him to and from gigs, which allowed him to indulge in his other hobby; sampling a few pints of real ale.

Geoff put the phone down and thought about Chloe, she was a 'mature' student but money never seemed to be a problem. Maybe she got some sort of grant for studying local history and archaeology at Lancaster University.

That was the easy part done, Geoff had rightly anticipated that he wouldn't get any serious grief when he told Wayne and Chloe about the cancellation but he knew that telling Lute would be a different 'kettle of fish.'

Geoff had known John Luther for as long as he could remember; John's family lived in one of the large private detached houses, on the opposite side of the road from Geoff's parents. They both attended the same primary school in Walton le Dale but their paths went separate ways when they were eleven years old and John went to the Grammar School in Preston where he was nicknamed 'Lute' by his contemporaries. It was a wonderful nick-name and Geoff was never sure whether it came about as a result of shortening John's surname or because of the fact that when most boys were yearning to play guitars, John got himself a Mandolin and became very proficient at playing it.

Lute had been married to Jackie for six years. Their four-year-old son, John junior, had drawn one of life's short straws; he was born with Down's syndrome. Jackie doted on him and no child anywhere in the world received such love and devoted attention.

The other three members of the band tried to understand the kind of problems caused by that sort of situation and accepted that Lute would just turn up and busk, leaving them to work out arrangements. This agreement certainly suited Geoff and the others. Lute had one hell of an artistic temperament and was an extremely difficult person to get along with. Although they were all in awe of his excellent musical ability, whether he was playing single-string vibrato, accompanying chords or lead breaks, they were glad that Lute was happy to turn up five minutes before the first spot, do his stuff and leave straight after the encore. If anyone questioned them about this arrangement they explained that it was because of his domestic situation, the truth of the matter was that they all thought that Lute, great musician or not, was a complete 'arsehole'.

On a recent gig Geoff had seen Lute taking some pills during the interval, Lute said they were for indigestion but they certainly didn't look like Rennies. Geoff tried to take the conversation further but Lute told him to "Mind his own business."

Although, to any outsiders looking in, the Luther household looked very comfortably off, the real truth of the matter was that Luther and Jackie were beginning to struggle financially. Six months earlier Lute had been made redundant. The synthetic textile company, that employed him as Assistant Quality Manager, had closed down due to competition from the Far East and although he was highly qualified, other companies were loathe to take him on. Whether this was because he had a severely disabled child who's urgent needs could drag him away from work at any time or whether it was his bitter and twisted attitude was questionable.

Jackie had been sick on the breakfast table that morning, not the best way to announce to your 'out of work' husband that you are pregnant, again.

Geoff dialled Lute's ex directory number. The phone rang for ages. Jackie's voice, sounding strained and tearful, came on the line.

"Hello."

"Hi Jackie it's Geoff, is Lute in?" Jackie didn't reply, the line went quiet for what seemed like an age. Geoff was about to hang up when he heard Lute's voice, "Sorry Geoff, you've caught us at a bad time, can it wait 'til tonight?"

"Actually Lute that's what I'm phoning about, tonight's been cancelled, Dougie reckons someone's bubbled him to the licensing people."

Geoff waited for a response, Lute sounded reasonably calm.

"Well Dougie booked it, invoice the fucker, he's got a contract with us."

Although Geoff knew that this was technically correct there was no way he was going to invoice Dougie for a cancellation fee.

"You know I can't do that Lute, Dougie's a mate and he's straight as a die, he wouldn't cancel if there was some way round it."

"Who the fucks doing this to us Geoff? I was relying on that fifteen quid, it's the only fucking income I've got coming in, Jackie's talking about fucking off and taking John with her! I'll tell you Geoff I'm getting really pissed off with this whole deal, I want it fucking sorting, OK!"

Even down the phone line Geoff could sense the stress in the voice, Lute could be prickly at the best of times but in all the years he'd known him he had never heard him swear.

"I can't prove it," said Geoff, "But I think its Charlie Bagwell from Super Nova who keeps putting the dagger in with the council. Frank Ross's sixties band are having the same problem, they've been cancelled in Clitheroe tonight and in Ribchester Friday." He went on, "If you're really stuck for the fifteen quid, I can lend it to you, pay me back when you can."

Geoff heard a sniffle, caused by a sharp intake of breath "Thanks Geoff but the way things are it's more like fifteen grand that I need to sort things out."

Geoff heard the click as Lute abruptly ended the call.

No sooner had Geoff replaced the handset, on his new cordless phone, than the electronic trill announced that someone was phoning him. He picked it up (half expecting it to be Lute calling back) and was surprised to hear a voice that he hadn't heard for a few years.

"Bloody hell mate you can fairly 'yap' on this phone - you've been engaged for nearly an hour."

"Brian! Long-time no see, How are you? How's Tina?"

"Fine, Fine, listen I've got a proposition for you, are you still looking for gigs?"

"Yeah, I've got a few in the book but we're having problems with cancellations. What have you got?"

"Listen Geoff, rather than talking about it over the phone, let's discuss it over a pint. I see it says in the Telegraph that your playing at the Brown Cow tonight, I'll pop in and see you there."

"Brown Cow's been cancelled Brian, Dougie phoned me this morning. How about we have one in the Shovel it's a bit quieter there and we could talk in private?"

"Sounds fine to me Geoff, is nine o clock OK?"

"Fine - I'll see you later then."

Chapter 2

Brian and Tina.

Geoff fiddled with the dial on the radio in an attempt to tune into BBC Radio Lancashire, he liked to spoil himself on a Saturday afternoon by relaxing in a hot herbal bath, listening to the second half commentary on the Preston North End match. He had decided that the set needed new batteries three weeks ago, when he had been listening to the Blackpool game, but he hadn't got round to actually buying any. Now the batteries had finally given up the ghost completely, he'd have to be happy with the results on TV later.

As he soaked in the warm water, which almost came up to his shoulders, Geoff started to think about Brian and wondered what he would have to say that evening.

Brian was a 'likeable rogue' but Geoff had a lot of time for him, in fact it was down to Brian that Geoff had developed an interest in folk singing. Brian had been a part of the 'Folk Revival' during the late sixties and early seventies; he'd regularly played at folk clubs and festivals, not only in Lancashire but also all over the country and, two or three times on the continent, in Holland and Sweden. He had also appeared regularly on BBC TV's Look North programme.

When he was at his peak, Brian never forgot that Folk Music was 'The music of the people' and he continued to support his local folk club whenever possible. In those days he could still be found, most Thursday evenings, at the Cromwell's Cave Folk Club, which convened in the upstairs room of the workingmen's club in Walton le Dale. He would be either hosting the evening or taking his turn, with the rest of the singers and musicians, who regularly turned up to play.

This was where Geoff had first met Brian and from then on they became good friends. Brian taught Geoff how to play the guitar and talked him into buying the best one he could afford. So off they went to Preston where Geoff bought a second-hand Martin Dreadnought for three hundred and forty nine pounds. The man in the music shop thought it strange that someone who could only play three chords, badly, was buying what was considered to be the best and most expensive acoustic guitar generally available.

Within six months Geoff was supporting Brian at some of his local gigs, he never actually got any payment for doing this and, looking back, it actually cost him because he always ended up paying for the beer. The routine went something like this: they would arrive at the gig and Geoff would get the beer in, a pint each for Brian and himself and a Cola for the long suffering Tina who was Brian's girlfriend (though on gigs he treated her more like a chauffeur). Geoff would then do his spot, usually about twenty minutes, during which time Brian would have extracted another pint from the organiser of the function. As soon as Geoff came off, Brian would get onto the stage, do his first number then 'down' what was left in his pint pot and signal to Geoff that he could do with another.

Geoff knew that Brian was taking advantage but he didn't mind one bit; lots of performers would give their right arm to be the support act at a Brian Clayton concert and play to a ready-made audience that was packed to the rafters. As far as Geoff was concerned supporting Brian was an experience that couldn't be bought for love or money. He was learning from the best and thoroughly enjoying every minute.

Geoff was never sure whether or not Tina enjoyed the concerts, she always maintained that she couldn't stand folk music and preferred listening to 'underground' rock music. When Brian was playing anywhere she would stay in the background and didn't seem to mind, when, during the interval or at the end of the evening, Brian was surrounded by most of the local single female population. Most of these lasses had got it into their heads that 'shagging a celebrity ' would put the icing on a good night out so Brian, and occasionally Geoff, became the target for their sexual advances.

Brian was a great flirt and had them all in the palm of his hand, snapping for the bait that he dangled their way but that was as far as it went, Geoff could not remember Brian ever being unfaithful to Tina during those wild and happy days. Tina was a product of the sixties and, at one time, certainly had the figure and the looks to parade in hot pants or micro skirt, tight blouses and a ton of mascara. But those days were gone and unfortunately Tina's figure was going after them but her mission in life was to keep up the image and continue with the look. Geoff had overheard a couple of well-oiled blokes talking in the gents' one night. The topic of conversation was 'Who they would and wouldn't like to shag'. One of them mentioned "The slag at the back with the corn-beef legs, big arse and droopy tits." Geoff knew they were talking about Tina.

The last time Geoff had seen Brian and Tina was at their wedding. That was a day to remember. Tina's dad owned a large chain of electrical goods shops plus most of the land in The Ribble Valley and was, to coin a phrase, rolling in it. Nothing would be too good for his daughter on her big day.

The service took place at Blackburn Cathedral and in the best traditions, of the now long-gone sixties, the place was awash with flower children handing out blooms. The huge congregation had been asked not to use paper confetti because rose petals were being provided to shower the newly wed couple when they left the church.

As well as the almost over-powering smell of roses, Geoff vividly remembered two other things about the service. Firstly, he'd thought that the whole thing was a bit OTT, considering that the couple were both in their late thirties. Secondly, he remembered the look on Brian's face when the folk singer had realised that the press photographers had turned up because this was the wedding of Frank Croxley's daughter and not local 'Folk singing celebrity' Brian Clayton.

The reception took place at the Prestigious Lord Derby Hotel, which was set in its own grounds just off the main drag between Whalley and Clitheroe. The wedding breakfast took place in the banqueting hall and all the guests were treated to a feast that was second to none. The bombshell came during Brian's well rehearsed 'groom's speech' when he announced publicly, there and then, that he was giving up performing and was going to spend the rest of his life keeping his beloved Tina in the manner to which she was accustomed. There were a few 'sharp intakes of breath' from the 'musos' who were at the function but the announcement was definitely getting the 'nod of approval' from the actual wedding party, who were sitting on the top table. Tina's Dad was grinning from ear to ear; her mother was nodding in agreement, though Geoff knew that the Polish woman would not like Brian referring to her beloved Christina as 'Tina' in public.

The fact that Stanislaw, Tina's twin brother, was Best Man had made Geoff suspect that maybe the stage-management of the wedding had not had any input from the folk singer. Brian couldn't abide Stan Croxley and always referred to him as 'That slimy twat'.

Geoff stood up in the now cool tub and reached over to the towel rail. He dried himself, slipped on a dressing gown and went into the parlour to catch the football results on TV. Preston had won; Blackburn and Blackpool had both lost. It was beginning to look like it could change into a good day after all.

Geoff had a couple of hours to kill before his rendezvous with Brian at the Malt Shovel; he flipped through his LPs to look for something relaxing and easy to listen to. He had almost worked his way to the back of the collection when his fingers stopped, there was Brian's face beaming at him, from the record sleeve. It was ages since he'd listened to one of Brian's albums. He took it out of the rack and placed it onto the turntable. Out of the hundreds of songs in Brian's repertoire, Geoff's favourite had always been the title track of this, Brian's best and last, album. Brian's songs usually consisted of traditional material of mainly Lancashire and Irish origin but, as far as Geoff knew, Brian had only ever written the one song himself, and had certainly only ever recorded the one. Geoff carefully dropped the stylus onto the outside edge of the black vinyl disc. He lay back, stretched

out prostrate on the settee and listened to Brian Clayton
singing 'The Rose of The Ribble Valley'.

Chapter 3

The Malt Shovel.

Geoff awoke with a start, it wasn't the record player stylus clicking away in the end groove of Brian's album that had woken him, it was something else. "RAT-A-TAT-TAT" there was someone banging on the front door. Geoff glanced at the clock it was twenty to nine "Shit! It's the taxi!" he thought. He shot to the door and opened it a couple of inches and saw a big beaming Asian smile.

"Sorry Ali, I was asleep Give me two minutes to pull some clothes on," said Geoff to the cheery taxi driver.

"Hurry up Sahib!" Joked Ali, in his best Karachi accent "or I'll be pleased to charge you waiting time."

Geoff knew that the driver was only joking; he often caught Geoff napping. Ali was not only his regular taxi driver but also a friend and a fan of Elderflower Punch. If Geoff and the band were playing anywhere local on his night off, then Ali would often pop in to see the show along with his girlfriend.

The taxi pulled up onto the normally quiet car park of The Malt Shovel, it was heaving, so much for the quiet rendezvous. Geoff paid Ali and gave him a tip and asked him to come back at midnight.

Geoff walked into the normally quiet pub and couldn't believe his eyes and ears. Gone were the old tables that consisted of formica covered plywood tops screwed on to the bases of old singer sewing machines. In their place were lots of white, pink and blue plastic chairs and tables. The walls had been covered by large, white fabric sheets that were stretched, tightly, over wooden frames to form large screens, which allowed beams of light to be projected onto them. The oscillating fans, fixed to the ceiling, above the screens, gently blew onto the fabric producing an effect of coloured lights dancing on ripples. The compact lighting rig, that was suspended, from the ceiling, illuminated the small stage that had been built in the corner of the room.

The music was almost deafening, Geoff could feel the bass notes rattling his rib cage. The last time he had experienced that sensation was when he sat on the front row at a 10CC concert in Preston Guildhall.

He instantly recognised the tune (he may have been a folk singer but he was a 'rocker' at heart) it was Ike and Tina Turner's *River Deep Mountain High*. Well 'almost' Ike and Tina Turner. Ike's guitar was certainly there, and the band was really rocking but Tina was way off key.

Geoff forced his way through the bodies to get a look at the band - what he saw when he managed to eventually get to the front beggared his belief.

Not a single musical instrument in sight and certainly no Ike. The only person on the stage was a redheaded lass of about 25 wearing a gold coloured bikini underneath a see-through dark blue chiffon cloak. She was gorgeous but Geoff wasn't paying any attention to her looks.

The only objects on the stage with her were the Shure microphone in her hand, and a footswitch on the floor in front of her. On each side of the stage there were two huge speaker stacks, each stack consisted of an eighteen-inch bass bin at the bottom, a twelve-inch mid-range cabinet in the middle and a large flared horn, for the treble, on the top. At the back of the stage was a rack-mounted sound system that consisted of two power amplifiers, a state of the art electronic reverb/echo unit, a six-channel mixer and a top of the range double cassette deck.

Geoff looked at it open mouthed, he wasn't as well up on this sort of thing as Wayne, but he figured that this woman had almost a thousand Watts-worth of sound power at her finger tips and not only that, she was coming through in glorious stereo. Elderflower Punch played through a one hundred Watt mono PA system and were often criticised for being too loud.

Geoff made his way over to the bar to see if Brian had arrived. On his way across the room he bumped into Dave and Julie Jackson who were two of Elderflower Punch's biggest followers, they went along to see Geoff and Co. whenever possible.

"What happened at the Brown Cow?" shouted Dave, in an attempt to be heard over the loud music "We've just come from there, it was heaving but Dougie said that he'd had to cancel,"

"He wouldn't tell us why," shouted Julie, "Someone said that there was music on here so we all came along to suss it out."

River Deep Mountain High suddenly came to an abrupt end with at least half a bar to go.

Geoff looked back at the singer; she was blushing with embarrassment

"I'd like to do an Abba song now," She said, with a nervous smile and a quiver in her voice. These were the only words she uttered before kicking the footswitch in front of her.

Every one in the place flinched as the last four notes of the Ike and Tina song boomed out through the speakers. There was a four-second silence then *Waterloo* kicked off, complete with Bjorn, Benny and Annifrid on the backing vocals. The girl came in with the main lyric half way through the first verse.

"Very professional backing band," shouted Dave sarcastically but no one could hear him above the, what could only be described as echoing racket. He put his mouth up to Geoff's ear and said, "I've just seen your old mate Brian Clayton in the bog, I've not seen him for ages. I thought he was out of the country; he's sitting in the vault."

Geoff nodded in acknowledgement and made his way through to the public bar.

It was considerably quieter in the vault although the regular 'darts and dominoes' crowd were all moaning about the noise coming through from next door.

"At least you can hear yourself think in here," thought Geoff. He glanced around the room and spotted Brian sitting at a table in the corner. He seemed to be in deep conversation with a bloke sat on the opposite side of the table, who had his back to Geoff.

Geoff made his way across to where his old friend sat. Brian looked up and a warm smile lit up his face. "Geoff" he said, "How goes it?" he stood up and thrust his hand into Geoff's. "You know Charlie?", he said.

The man who Brian had been talking with was none other than Charlie Bagwell, the unscrupulous proprietor of The Super Nova Entertainment Agency.

"We've met!" said Geoff avoiding the handshake offered by Bagwell.

"Still playing Geoff? I wouldn't have thought that your band could afford to take a Saturday night off!" said Bagwell sarcastically.

"Everyone needs a break Charlie," said Geoff, smiling to himself as he pictured, in his mind's eye, Bagwell in plaster of Paris from head to toe.

"What did you think of Vera Lynne next door then?" asked Brian jokingly.

"That's Velvet," said Bagwell, "She's got a big future in this game!"

Geoff couldn't resist rising to the challenge, "She's got big tits and a big arse too - pity she can't bloody sing!"

Brian smiled.

"I'm not staying here listening to this twat. He wouldn't know talent if it came and bit him on the bollocks." Said Charlie, "See you Brian."

"You're a nothing but a slime-ball Bagwell," said Geoff "You and your sort are killing live music."

"Just a minute Charlie," said Brian as the agent rose to leave. He then turned and spoke to the folksinger, "Geoff I'm just going to get something from Charlie's car, I'll be back in a minute, get the ale in, I'm on bitter."

Same old Brian thought Geoff; no doubt Bagwell had paid for the half-drunken pint still on the table in front of Brian's seat.

Geoff pushed his way to the bar and ordered two pints of bitter. "Sorry!" said the barmaid "No proper glasses left." The flat, headless beer was served in two plastic pint tumblers.

Brian came back in with a handful of Super Nova leaflets, which he rolled up and put into his pocket. "It's too bloody noisy to talk about anything here Geoff" said Brian "I've just phoned Tina, she's coming to pick us up in fifteen minutes, we'll go back to our place." After sampling the weak, tasteless beer in the plastic 'glass', Geoff was quietly pleased with this proposition.

They downed their pints and went outside to wait for Tina. Brian said that she didn't like walking into pubs on her own. Geoff smiled as he thought to himself "She's probably sick of waiting for her husband to buy her a drink."

A beige colored Jaguar XJ6 with the registration T1 NAS pulled up on the car park. Tina got out and walked across to hug Geoff. He noticed that she hadn't changed that much, not in the fashion department anyway unless of course the black fishnet tights were just a half-hearted attempt to hide the cellulite that had formed on her thighs.

Chapter 4

Dunstrummin.

The Jaguar purred along at about forty-five miles an hour. Geoff knew from past experience, that, when driving, Tina was always careful, some would say 'slow.' It was maximum speed limit on this road but Tina wouldn't put her foot down. Geoff remembered the old days when the couple, on their way to a gig, would pick him up in Brian's Vauxhall Viva Estate, Brian drove to the gigs Tina drove home, Tina would never travel faster than fifty miles per hour, even on the motorway.

Less than four miles from the pub, Tina indicated left and turned off onto a side road that was signed: -

PRIVATE ROAD

NO ENTRY TO UNAUTHORISED VEHICLES

The road surface was immaculate, although not smooth; it had been constructed from cobble sets, probably recycled from the old roads of Preston & Blackburn. Twenty yards up the track they came upon a pair of intimidating wrought iron gates. Tina stopped the Jag and wound down the window. She removed the ignition keys and pointed the fob at the gates; they opened silently.

There was a large sign on the right hand gatepost it said: -

CROXLEY ESTATE
NO ENTRY TO UNAUTHORISED PERSONS.
TRADESMEN PLEASE CONFIRM ARRIVAL ON
INTERCOM BEFORE PROCEEDING

The gates closed automatically as they passed through them. The cobbled road continued for a mile or so, gently climbing through the heavily wooded countryside.

Brian hadn't said much during the journey, probably because he couldn't get a word in, Tina was wanted to know everything that Geoff had been up to since last time they'd met. Was he still playing? Did he still live in that quaint end terraced house? Was there a special lady in his life and if not why not? All the usual stuff that old friends discuss.

The Jag pulled over the brow at the top of the hill. Geoff was gob-smacked; they went through an archway into the courtyard of what could only be described as a mansion. "Jesus," thought Geoff, "it makes Samlesbury Hall look like a council house."

Brian turned around and smiled at his back seat passenger's astonished look "Don't panic Geoff, that's where the in-laws live, our pad's a bit further on."

They crossed the courtyard and exited through a similar arch on the far side. The cobbled drive now turned into plain old tarmac and after another hundred yards or so Tina pulled up outside a small but very impressive cottage. The stone walls were painted white, there was a thatched roof, a smoking chimney pot and an old fashioned porch at the front door. The sign on the wall took the shape of a guitar with the neck broken and hanging down. On the body of the guitar in gold letters outlined in black was the name of the cottage: -

DUNSTRUMMIN

Brian opened the back door of the car to allow his guest to get out. Tina walked up the two steps to the cottage and went in, Geoff noticed that the door hadn't been locked. Brian stood on the step, as if on ceremony and waved Geoff forward saying, "Welcome to my castle!"

"Our castle!" shouted Tina, in an authoritative but humorous voice.

"You know what they say about an English-man's home love," said Brian with a smile.

The inside of the cottage was just as impressive as the exterior. The walls and ceiling were 'rough plastered' but finished off in a warm beige emulsion that had been expertly applied to the gaps in between the dark brown wooden beams. There was a log fire crackling away in the hearth of a rustic sandstone fireplace. The furniture was perfect for a small cottage. There was a floral covered three-piece suite, the settee of which, due to the size of the room, only had room for two, and an old oak dining table with three chairs over in the corner.

The only 'mod con' that Geoff could see was a small TV set in the corner. It seemed strange, considering Brian's musical background, that there wasn't a stereo unit in the room.

Brian sat down at the table and motioned Geoff to join him.

"Tea, coffee or beer?" asked Tina

"It is Geoff, remember?" Said Brian "Don't waste your time with tea and coffee love!"

Tina got the message, she left the room and came back with a large silver tray and put it down on the table. It contained a large plate of crackers along with a cheese-board with at least a pound of 'Lancashire' on it, a slab of best butter and two pewter beer mugs, both empty. "Don't panic Geoff we've got plenty to put in them." Said Tina, smiling as she made her way back to the door.

She returned with four-pint cans and placed them in the centre of the table "Help yourself," said Brian.

"Cheers Tina" said Geoff.

Geoff took a can and looked at the label as he levered back the ring-pull 'Samuel Brown's Northern Bitter.' It wouldn't have been Geoff's personal choice, if he had been providing the booze. Although the Best Bitter that Browns sold in their pubs was excellent by any standards, Northern Bitter was a much weaker brew that could be sold reasonably cheaply in local off-licences and compete, price-wise, with the supermarkets' own brands which were very cheap but weak and tasteless.

"Never mind" thought Geoff, he needed a clear head if he was to talk business and this was the first time ever that he could remember drinking with Brian and not paying for the beer.

"Well," said Brian, "I suppose you're wondering what this is all about?"

"I was kind of hoping that you'd get round to it" Geoff replied with a smile.

"I want you come and be one of the resident bands at my pub," said Brian.

"Your pub!" exclaimed Geoff "Which bloody pub?"

"The Grey Mare," said Brian; "Tina and I are moving into the licensed trade."

"Where's the Grey Mare?" enquired Geoff.

"It doesn't exist yet," said Brian, "But it will in a few weeks time." He went on: "Do you remember doing a gig at the old Convent Bowling Club down by the river?"

"Vaguely," said Geoff.

"Well it became derelict and closed about two years ago, apparently there's some planning clause in the deeds that says that the premises, or anything built on the land, can only be used for recreational purposes. Tina's old man owns it and decided to do something with it so he's knocking the old clubhouse down and building a pub in its place."

"So you're going to run it for him then?"

"Not exactly run it! He's bought it as a joint fiftieth birthday present for Tina and me; reckons it's about time we got our teeth into a business."

"I can't see you and Tina settling down to life serving chicken in the basket and pints of bitter-shandy."

"That's why I needed to talk to you Geoff!"

Brian went on to explain that Tina and he fully intended The Grey Mare to become the best 'live music venue' in the area. Tina would look after the food and drink side of things while he sorted out the entertainment. He aimed to cater for all musical tastes with local talent hosting Folk, Blues, Country, Rock, and Jazz on different nights of the week with bigger named artistes appearing on Saturdays. He wanted Geoff, either on his own or with his band, to run the Folk Night, which was going to be on Sundays (Brian had done his homework, there were no other regular folk-nights on a Sunday within a fifty mile radius).

Geoff enquired about the money and Brian said that he had a budget of twenty-five pounds per week for the folk-night. Currently the band were going out 'locally' for a minimum of fifty quid, at weekends. Geoff had already worked out that if he ran the most of the nights himself, and had the band with him on the first Sunday in every month he wouldn't be out of pocket and the band wouldn't get bored with the routine, they rarely got booked on Sundays anyway. He put the suggestion to Brian who was happy with the idea.

Brian had arranged for Frank Ross from Clitheroe to run the 'Rock Night' on Friday and the Jazz band that had been barred from playing at The Weaver's Institute due to the licensing problem would do Jazz on Wednesdays. He had some ideas for candidates for the 'Blues Night' and the 'Country Night' but nothing was finalised.

The enthusiasm in the continuing discussion was a certain sign that both Brian and Geoff were excited about the forthcoming project at The Grey Mare.

Geoff looked at his watch; it was quarter past eleven. He thought about Ali and the Taxi; "Brian, can I use your phone? I've a taxi booked for midnight but he thinks I'm at The Shovel"

"Sure said Brian, "Ask him to come here, tell him to use the intercom at the gate."

Tina butted in "There's no closing time here, tell your driver to make it one o'clock."

Geoff phoned the taxi Company they told him that Ali would be there shortly after one.

"Fancy another can?" said Brian

"Yeah, cheers!" said Geoff not over enthusiastically.

"Not keen on the old Sammy Browns then Geoff?"

"It's OK but I've tasted better."

"We'll see what we can do then, Tina fetch the jar and the jug."

Brian crossed to the hearth, picked up the poker and thrust it into the glowing embers of the fire.

Tina brought a quart earthenware jug and a small stoneware jar and placed them on the table. The jar was about five inches high, and three inches in diameter. It had a neatly fitting lid but the most striking thing about the jar was decorated with a pewter rose halfway down the outside.

Brian removed the lid and Geoff became aware of a faint smell of roses, it reminded him of the confetti at Brian and Tina's wedding. Brian dipped his finger and thumb into the jar and grasped a small pewter scoop that was about teaspoon size. He scooped out some of the contents, it looked like dried pink flower petals. Brian put them into the palm of his hand and rubbed both hands together over the top of the jug. This pulverised the petals, which he then allowed to fall into the vessel below.

Geoff was spellbound as he watched.

Tina cracked open two cans of Sammy Browns and poured them slowly into the jug, then she took the jug in both hands and moved it in a circular motion making the liquid, inside, swirl around.

Geoff panicked a bit: "If that's some sort of dope you can leave me out of it," he said. Although something told him it wasn't, he had never known Brian to dabble in drugs.

"A secret old Croxley family concoction," said Brian, "made from the petals of roses that grow in the woods out back; doesn't half make old Sammy Brown taste good."

Brian pulled the poker out of the fire and thrust the red-hot glowing tip into the jug. There was a hissing noise and quite a bit of steam. The room was almost instantly filled with the most amazing aroma; it was like walking through a rose garden in full bloom on a still, warm summer's evening.

Brian poured the, now warm, beer into the pewter tankards and handed one to Geoff.

"Your health!" he said as he held his tankard up towards Geoff.

"Cheers" said Geoff. They touched tankards and downed the contents.

Geoff felt marvellous, not only did the brew taste superb; it was as if suddenly the weight of the whole world had been lifted off his shoulders.

The conversation turned to the good old days when Brian was gigging regularly and Geoff was doing the support. They laughed as they discussed, with affection, the venues and some of the characters that they had met therein. Geoff couldn't remember being so laid back and relaxed in a long time.

They were disturbed by a loud triple beep; Tina looked like she was talking to the wall. It was the intercom. "It's your taxi," she said "He'll be up here in five minutes."

Brian grabbed Geoff's leather jacket and passed it to him. They were both still laughing after recalling the events that had followed a sudden power cut during a gig at Knowle Green Village Hall.

Geoff finally plucked up the courage to ask the question that he had avoided all night. "Brian, when you eventually get these music nights up and running, will you be coming out of retirement and giving us a song or two?"

Tina was clearing the table, putting everything back onto the large silver tray. Geoff sensed that she had stopped what she was doing and was waiting to see how Brian reacted to the question.

"Like it says on the sign Geoff, 'Dunstrummin,' that's me!" Tina carried on with the task in hand.

"Pity," said Geoff "You're still the best you know, you'd still pull them in from miles around." He went on: "I realised what was missing, from the local scene, when I listened to one of your old albums today."

"Really," said Brian "Which one?"

"The Rose of The Ribble Valley," said Geoff.

There was a loud ear-splitting crash when the tray that Tina dropped hit the floor. Geoff noticed that she had tears in her eyes when she ran quickly out of the room.

Almost instantly there was a knock on the door. "That'll be your taxi," said Brian.

"I hope Tina's OK," said Geoff.

"She has funny turns like that," said Brian "I just hope she's not pregnant!" he said with a laugh.

Ali knocked again. Geoff made his way out to the taxi. "Goodnight," said Brian, "I'll be in touch."

Chapter 5

Dreaming.

Ali set off back through the courtyard and down the cobbled track. "You're going up in the world," said Ali "Socialising with the Croxleys."

Geoff was explaining about Brian and how he had married into the family when, suddenly, the gates appeared in front of them. Ali slowed down and flashed his headlights four times in quick succession. The gates opened as if by magic. Ali smiled at Geoff, "It works going out but you've got to use the intercom coming in."

"How did you know about that?" asked Geoff.

"I come from a long line of Fakirs," joked Ali, "Opening locked gates comes naturally to us, just like charming snakes, climbing up unsupported ropes and lying on beds of nails."

"Smart-arse!" said Geoff.

"Actually," said Ali, "I go up there every Wednesday to pick up Mrs. Clayton and drive her to her clinic over in Preston."

"Clinic! What is she, some sort of Therapist?" Asked Geoff.

"No! Actually she's some sort of patient," said Ali, "I take her to see a private shrink."

Geoff wondered if that explained Tina's strange behaviour just before he left.

Ali turned out of the drive and onto the road. For the next half-mile or so they drove along next to a high stone wall that bordered the highway. It surrounded a vast expanse of mature woodland. Locals referred to it as 'Croxley's Wood' though the Ordnance Survey maps recorded the relatively large green patch as 'The Lirium'. At the halfway point a pair of large solid wooden gates had been fitted across a break in the wall. The ivy growing up them, the weedy scrub growing in front and huge tarnished brass lock on a rusty hasp and staple suggested that they hadn't been opened for years.

33

"Always looks like a spooky kind of a place to me," said Ali as he noticed Geoff looking at the woods "have you ever been inside?"

"No," said Geoff, "But I remember a few years ago there was a bunch of hippies, who were up this way protesting about the woods on the other side of the road, being destroyed to make way for the dual carriage-way. They climbed over the gates and camped in there. When the coppers went in to throw them out, they were all high as fucking kites, the drug squad went in and found nothing." He laughed out loud as he pictured the scene: a dozen or so semi-naked hippies dancing around a group of very embarrassed policemen complete with Alsatian dogs. Ali smiled to himself as he looked at the inebriated Geoff, "Must be something in the air in these parts!" he said.

The taxi had to slow down to give way, as a large lorry started to pull out of a transport depot. 'F CROXLEY & SON' was the name on the sign outside the gates.

Frank Croxley never had enough confidence in his son, Stan, to let him get involved in the retail side of the business so he found him the position as Director of the transport and warehouse side of things. Being in charge of that part of the operation took practically no brains at all and in reality a chap named Lawrie Jackson, the Transport Manager, was running it. Frank's motive for looking after Stan in this way was that 'dear Stanislaw' was the last male of the Croxley bloodline.

Ali's headlights illuminated the side of the lorry, on it where the words: -

RIBBLE VALLEY ELECTRICS

The words formed a semi-circle around the bottom of a large red heraldic Lancashire rose. This reminded Geoff of Brian's song; he started to hum the tune.

Geoff was still humming when Ali pulled up outside the door of the end-terraced house; Geoff paid him, plus tip, and went inside.

As always the Martin was stood up safely in the guitar stand at one side of the room. Geoff still had the song floating about his head, he had never actually tried to play it before; it was, after all, Brian's song. What the hell! If Brian really had 'dunstrummin', the song was there for the taking. He took the guitar and started to strum and sing it. It must have been the effects of the Sammy Brown's; his co-ordination had gone completely out of the window.

He went to bed.

Lying there, in those twilight moments between consciousness and sleep, Geoff imagined he could smell roses; his subconscious was still humming 'The Rose of the Ribble Valley.'

He drifted off into a deep relaxed sleep and his mind started to work overtime, Geoff was not usually prone to vivid, memorable dreams but the one on which he was he was now embarking was a real Oscar winner.

He was in the midst of a woodland, the dense foliage above was blocking out the most of the light, but where the sunshine had managed to squeeze its way through the gaps in the leafy cover, it produced a very dramatic effect indeed. Bright shafts of white light projected straight down to the woodland floor from the canopy above, each shaft was animated by a myriad of small flying insects that were looking for warmth and light.

Geoff was sitting on a log in a glade that was free from trees. The woodland floor around him was covered with low growing bracken. Around the edge of the glade was an almost impenetrable wall consisting of large tree trunks, the space in between was filled with wild rose bushes growing about six-feet high and every one of them almost completely covered in beautiful, fragrant pink roses. The perfume was almost overpowering.

Geoff was strumming away singing 'The Rose of the Ribble Valley' but he didn't have the Martin with him, he was playing on what looked very much like Lute's Mandolin.

Many of the inquisitive woodland creatures had ventured to the edge of the glade to listen to the soothing music and see what sort of animal was producing this sound. There were owls, foxes, badgers, rabbits, deer and some animals that only existed in dreams.

Geoff was singing the last of the five verses when he realised that human eyes were also watching him. There was a figure, in the shadow at the far end of the glade. Geoff finished the song but carried on strumming the mandolin, it felt as if some strange but irresistible force had taken over the movement of his arms and hands.

The mysterious figure stepped forward into a shaft of sunlight. It was a girl!

Geoff was mesmerised by the flaxen-haired beauty illuminated before him. Despite her frugal attire, she was the most alluring creature he had ever set his eyes upon. She wore a plain brown sackcloth robe that was tied around her waist with a frayed chord and around her neck, hanging on a leather thong, was a pewter rose pendant, just like the one on Brian's jug.

Geoff couldn't stop strumming the chord sequence and was astonished when the girl sang another verse. She sang as if the song belonged to her, the verse certainly did, as far as Geoff knew, Brian had only written the five.

As soon as the girl finished singing, the force, whatever it was, released its grip and he stopped playing. He smiled at the girl; she beckoned him to follow and walked into a gap between two trees.

Geoff put down the instrument and followed.

The girl never slowed down enough to allow him to catch up and although the woodland was dense the narrow footpath that the girl appeared to be following, was quite well defined as it wound its way downwards through the trees.

The tree cover was getting thinner, and the sound of birdsong, which had accompanied him since he started to follow the girl, died away and was replaced by a loud gurgling sound He was following the southern bank of the River Ribble in an up stream direction. He was fifty yards or so behind the girl. The area was somehow familiar to him.

A stone-built wall surrounded a group of daunting looking buildings ahead of him. It seemed strange that although the wall looked strong enough to keep out an army, there was an entrance way built into it that didn't appear to have any gates or other means of keeping out unwelcome visitors. The girl went through the gap in the wall and Geoff followed her a few seconds later. He had to give way to four silent, black robed, nuns who were leaving the place, their hands clasped firmly together and their covered heads bent in prayer.

He stepped through the gap and found himself in an enclosed grassed area. He spotted the girl on the far side; she was stood by a mound of earth that had a plain wooden cross erected at one end of it.

Geoff made his way across to the girl. As he got closer she put out her hands as if she wished to embrace him. When their eyes met her expression suddenly changed to one of alarm. "You are not Bryan of Clayton!" She said.

"BONG" the bell in the tower of one of the buildings rang out loudly, the girl fled, "BONG - BONG" the sound of the bell was deafening it threw Geoff into a state of confusion, "BONG - BONG - chirp - chirp - bong - CHIRP - CHIRP. Geoff opened his eyes, the phone by the bed was ringing out. He glanced at the clock as he reached for the receiver.

It was nine forty-five

"Hello."

"Geoff, It's Chloe, I'm with Wayne, Lute's dead! Can we come over?"

Geoff felt a sudden sense of shock, brought on by both Chloe's phone call and the fragrant pink rose that had mysteriously appeared on the pillow beside him.

Chapter 6

Bad news.

Geoff dressed quickly and went downstairs to tidy the parlour. If Wayne had been coming alone he probably wouldn't have bothered, but because Chloe was coming and Chloe was a woman, he felt that he had to work on making the place look at least presentable.

He put the mysterious rose into a wineglass and placed it on top of the TV set.

The kettle was switched on and the tea bag was in the cup, two slices of thick brown bread were in the toaster and although still shocked by the bad news, Geoff couldn't stop thinking about his dream, particularly the girl and the extra verse in the song. Try as he might he couldn't remember the words to the extra verse that the girl had sung, but they had been 'real' enough all right, real as the rose that appeared on the pillow.

Geoff decided to put the whole episode out of his mind and tried to convince himself that it was all due to the effect of Brian's herbal beer.

Chloe and Wayne arrived. Geoff made tea; more appropriate than the usual beer, he thought, under the circumstances. The three of them sat in the parlour; Wayne looked pale and in shock, Chloe's eyes were bright red and she clutched a handkerchief that was saturated with tears, tightly in her hand.

Geoff was not comfortable in these sorts of situations, he never knew what to say or when to say it. However, he had to break the ice because it was obvious that the other two were in some sort of shock and probably assumed that he already knew the details. "What happened?" he said.

Chloe burst into tears.

"The stupid bastard!" said Wayne "He broke into the offices at Super Nova, slashed his wrists and bled to death all over Charlie Bagwell's desk."

"Jesus" said Geoff, not knowing whether he meant it as a prayer or a profanity.

He flashed back to the dream and pictured the grave with the wooden cross. Had it been some sort of premonition? No! It wasn't Lute in that particular grave.

Chloe wiped her nose and attempted to dry her tears with the soaking wet handkerchief Geoff went to the kitchen and brought back a roll of paper towel and handed it to Chloe.

"Sorry," he said, "My budget doesn't run to tissues."

"Oh Geoff! We've all said such horrible things about him and now he's gone," said Chloe bursting into tears again.

Geoff suddenly remembered what his mother used to do in situations like this and went for a bottle of Whisky that had been hiding, unopened, in the cupboard at the bottom of the bookcase, since Christmas. "Do you want it straight, or in your tea?" he said to the others.

They both elected to have the whisky in their tea; it certainly did the trick and despite the dour circumstances the trio relaxed.

"I was speaking to Bagwell in The Shovel last night," said Geoff "He obviously didn't know anything about it then."

"No said Chloe, he called in at the office on his way home and walked in on Lute." She went on "Lute was still breathing, Bagwell did what he could but he was dead when the ambulance arrived. If Bagwell had turned up five minutes earlier, he may have been in time to save him."

Geoff shivered as he thought about last night's discussion with Charlie Bagwell. "I was arguing with Bagwell just before he left. If I'd let it go he could have been there earlier."

"Don't blame yourself Geoff," said Wayne, "You weren't to know and neither was Charlie."

"Who told you about this? Has it been on the radio or something?" asked Geoff.

"Jackie's sister, Sue, phoned me," said Chloe "she's round at the house consoling Jackie, it must have been a terrible shock for her."

Geoff couldn't help thinking that it must have been horrendous for Bagwell too. He regarded the bloke as a complete 'shit-house' but wouldn't have wished that upon him, whether the body belonged to Lute or a complete stranger.

Chloe went on. "She phoned, to let me know, in case we had a gig imminent. Jackie didn't know, apparently her and Lute hadn't been talking for a few weeks and although she didn't go into detail, Sue said that Lute was in dire straits financially."

"Tell me about it," said Geoff, he told them about the previous day's phone call and the episode with the pills.

"Looks like last night's cancellation was the straw that broke the camels back," Said Wayne "So the stupid prick went and took it out on Bagwell."

Chloe began to cry again, she glared at Wayne, "I think you could refer to John with a little more respect," she said.

Geoff picked up on the 'John'; it was a long time since he had heard anyone refer to Lute by his real name.

"Come off it Chloe," said Wayne, "He may have been a bloody good musician but he was an obnoxious, pretentious pillock."

The tears came on stronger, "Yes, but he's dead now so that doesn't matter anymore, he was a member of our band, what are we going to do?"

"We can always go out as trio until we find someone else," said Geoff.

"Stay as a trio!" said Wayne; "Why bother finding someone else."

"You insensitive pair of bastards!" exclaimed Chloe, in a most uncharacteristic outburst. "I don't mean what will the band do, as regards playing? I mean what are we going to do for Lute."

"What do you suggest we do, commission a fucking statue?" said Wayne sarcastically.

"Hang on a minute Wayne, she's got a point," said Geoff "We may not have always seen eye to eye with Lute's point of view but as Chloe says, he was a member of the band."

"Sorry Chloe" said Wayne "It's just that I'm having trouble coping with all this."

"It's OK Wayne! We all are."

"Seriously then Chloe, What do you think we should do?" asked Geoff.

"Well first of all I want a fiver off each of you so that I can order some nice flowers and a card from the band. I'll sort that out and I think that all three of us should go to the funeral. Then we should organise a 'benefit concert' to raise a few pounds for young John."

"That's a nice thought Chloe," said Geoff "I'll sort out a venue A.S.A.P."

"Talking of venues," said Wayne, "What about the Hog's Head on Saturday? Are we going ahead with it, or do you think that, under the circumstances, we should cancel?"

Chloe was adamant "Go ahead with it, Lute would have wanted the show to go on."

The two men agreed and were both secretly glad that Chloe was there to get them organised. They liked her next touch too; she filled three tumblers with whisky and proposed a toast to Lute. Not a bad gesture, from someone who usually drank fruit juice.

The alcohol helped to release their inhibitions. Geoff got some cans of beer, for Wayne and himself. Chloe went back to having fruit juice.

"Here's a blast from the past," said Wayne, picking up the album sleeve that was leaning against the stereo system, "Brian Clayton!"

"Yes," said Geoff "I was listening to it yesterday, I went for a drink, with Brian, last night."

"I thought he was long gone," said Wayne.

"No, not at all, it's just that he hung up his guitar when he got married He still lives local, in fact him and Tina live in a cottage on her fathers estate."

"Who's her father?" said Chloe, suddenly showing an interest in the conversation

"Frank Croxley" said Geoff "He owns Ribble Valley Electrics as well as most of the land round here.

"I know of him," said Chloe, "I'm involved on a dig on some of his land at the moment, he's about to build a pub on the sight of an old derelict bowling club, down by the river."

"That's an incredible coincidence," said Geoff. He explained about Brian's project and how he wanted Geoff and the band to be involved.

The other two seemed happy with the proposed, preliminary arrangement of Geoff hosting the Sunday night with the band playing once a month. Until he had further discussions, with Brian, that was all he could tell them but now something at the back of his mind was niggling him.

"Why the interest in that particular site?" Asked Geoff.

"Our studies indicate that it was once the sight of a monastery" said Chloe "and the fact that it was called 'The Convent Bowling Club' and lies at the bottom of Monkswood Lane sort of backs the theory up."

Geoff sat bolt upright, he flashed-back to the conversation at Dunstrummin the previous night and his sub-conscious was forming images of the buildings and the grave that had featured, so vividly, at the end of his dream. Were the buildings in his vision and the old Convent Bowling Club at the same location?

"What exactly are you digging for?" asked Geoff

"That's part of the attraction of being a local historian come archaeologist," said Chloe "You don't always know what you are looking for until you find it." She went on: "So far at the Monkswood sight we've unearthed what we believe to be part of the foundations of the monastery. The complex appears to have been surrounded by a stone wall that may have been some sort of fortification. It appears that the clubhouse itself was built on the foundation of the original building; we will be able to confirm that when it's demolished next week. We would like to do some digging on the two bowling greens but your Mr Croxley has forbidden it."

"Why's that?" asked Wayne.

"Since the Clubhouse closed down, because it was deemed unsafe a couple of years ago, some of the old members still use the greens. They have maintained the greens themselves, and to be honest they've kept them in tip-top condition. I'd be bloody upset if someone wanted to come and dig them up."

Geoff interrupted, "What happened to the people who lived at the monastery then, why did they leave?"

"Ah!" said Chloe "That's down to your Mr Croxley, or should I say Mr Croxley's ancestor, only in those days it was Croxleigh, spelt L-E-I-G-H - Sir Frederick Croxleigh, who was a bit of a tyrant by all accounts. Apparently he acquired the land in a wager, the monks had left some years earlier and the building was being used as a convent by an order of nuns, for reasons best known to himself Croxleigh threw the nuns off his land."

"Sounds like a nice bloke" said Geoff.

"There's not too much known about him or the family, except that they lost their title due to some indiscretion, hence the subtle change in the spelling of the surname."

"What was the indiscretion?" asked Wayne. "I'm not totally sure," said Chloe "but I think that there was some sort of incest involved."

Chapter 7

Farewell to a fellow musician.

The night at the Hog's Head came and went. The three remaining members of Elderflower Punch felt a little strange performing without Lute and asked the audience to join them in a 'minute's silence' before they started to play. There was a good crowd in the pub and every single person respected the request and kept quiet for the whole sixty seconds. The landlord, after hearing through the 'grapevine' that the band intended to put on a benefit night, kindly raffled a bottle of whisky during the interval and gave the proceeds, which came to thirty five pounds, to Chloe so that she could add it to the total raised. Despite the sombre atmosphere the three of them played well, as a trio, much to the delight of audience and publican alike.

Due to the inevitable inquest, Lute's funeral was delayed until a week the following Thursday. Chloe had arranged to pick up the two men and drive them to the church, then on to the crematorium.

After the service the three of them joined the traditional line of people who wanted to express their condolences to the widow. Jackie put her arms around Geoff and hugged him.

"Thanks for coming Geoff, It's nice to know that there are some folks here who actually cared about Lute."

Geoff looked puzzled.

She went on: "Twelve years working in that factory and not one of the buggers came today, they never sent anyone round to see me or even sent a card."

Geoff had a good idea why that was the case; he couldn't help thinking that if Lute had been as prickly with his ex work colleagues as he was with members of the band, then they would have good reason not to get involved. He patted young John on the head; "Look after your mum," he said and turned to leave.

"Hang on Geoff," said Jackie "I've laid on a buffet and a few drinks at home, Susan's done a lovely spread. It would mean a lot to John and me if you three would come back and join us."

Chloe and Wayne both said they had prior arrangements. Chloe was still up to her neck in the Monkswood Lane project and had an appointment with someone from Whalley Abbey who kept records and may be able to throw some light on to the goings on at the old monastery and convent. Wayne said he had to practice with the Jazz Band. Geoff knew this wasn't true but he suspected that Wayne had his own reasons for not wanting to go.

Geoff asked Chloe to drop him at home so that he could pick up his car. He put his guitar in the boot and drove to Lute's house in Walton le Dale.

Lute's mother was at the house; he'd seen her at the church, with Lute's Father who had elected not to attend the after service get-together for drinks and sandwiches. Geoff knew from old that Lute's father was a staunch military type and would probably consider suicide as the act of a coward.

Geoff spent most of the time chatting with Jackie's sister, Sue. She often came along to watch the band; Wayne always joked that she was spying on Lute and making sure that he wasn't bothering with other women. Geoff knew different. Sue had often offered him a lift home after a gig; it usually resulted in her popping in for a nightcap and leaving sometime after breakfast.

It was about seven o'clock when the guests started to leave. Before saying his goodbyes to Jackie and young John, Geoff asked Sue if she fancied popping in to The Cromwell's Cave Folk Club with him. The club convened every Thursday at the workingmen's club in Walton le Dale. She declined saying that she felt Jackie would need her company that night. Geoff agreed with her.

He was feeling awkward about what he should say to Jackie and John junior before he left and was relieved when Jackie took the initiative.

"Thanks again for coming Geoff, it really does mean a lot. I know that Lute wasn't the easiest person to get along with but he was a good man where it counted, with John and me. We were all doing fine until the damn redundancy, he couldn't cope with the thought that he might not be able to provide for us."

"I know that," said Geoff; "whenever he came along to play with the band he never hung about for drinks or after-gig parties, he always wanted to get back home to you and John."

"Music was his escape Geoff, the rest of his time was dedicated to John junior and his job at the factory. It was a real blow to him when the place closed down. The Doctor put him on tranquillisers a couple of weeks later, he was taking them right up to the end." Jackie started to cry again. "Those bloody pills; Lute may have died a fortnight ago but I lost my husband six months ago when that bloody factory closed down."

Geoff put his arms around her to try and console her. "Jackie, Lute would have wanted you to be strong for young John's sake." It seemed the right thing to say at the time and seemed to do the trick.

Jackie stopped crying and composed herself. "There's something I need to talk to you about before you go." She beckoned Geoff to follow and led him into a side room which, from its appearance, had been Lute's office come den. Resting on three instrument stands in the corner were Lute's mandolin plus a guitar and a tenor banjo. All three of them were quality instruments. Gibson made the guitar and mandolin and Geoff knew that Lute had commissioned the banjo from a Luthier who lived over in Kirkham. Geoff had not seen either the banjo or the guitar before.

Jackie said, "They were his pride and joy Geoff. He always said if anything ever happened to him, make sure they go to a good home and make sure that someone in that home is a musician and will play them. I know how much they're worth Geoff; I would appreciate it if you could try and find buyers for the guitar and the banjo, I'll put the money in John's trust fund. I'd like you to have the mandolin!"

" I couldn't!" said Geoff, embarrassed; "I'm only a novice on mandolin and it must be worth hundreds of pounds."

"Geoff I'll be happy, and I'm sure that, wherever he is, Lute will be more than happy in the knowledge that you are perfecting your mandolin playing skills on the best instrument available. Take it and enjoy it and whenever you're playing it think about the three of us and remember the happy times."

"Thanks Jackie!" He said, "I'll always treasure it."

"Can you take the guitar and banjo with you as well? They will only remind me of Lute." She added, "Oh and take the stands too."

"No problem," said Geoff "I'm sure I won't have any problem finding good homes for them and when I do I'll bring the money round." He patted young John on the head and left the house taking the instruments with him.

Chapter 8

Cromwell's Cave.

Geoff pulled up onto the car park of the Walton le Dale workingmen's club. The Cromwell's Cave Folk Club met here, in an upstairs room, each Thursday at eight-thirty PM. It was the longest running folk club in the area and all types of acoustic music were encouraged. The present organisers of the club where Steve and Carol Whalley; a husband and wife team, who performed together in a duo known as Pushing Forté. They were excellent hosts with an almost inexhaustible collection of contemporary and traditional songs in their repertoire. Steve was the front man, with a great line in patter; he played a Yamaha guitar. Carol played the Irish drum and tambourine and the pair both sang in close harmony with each other.

Geoff opened his boot and took out his guitar and Lute's mandolin. If he was going to start playing it, now was as good a time as any. He left Lute's guitar and banjo plus the stands locked in the boot, happy that they were safely out of sight from any would-be thieves who may be about. The Krook-Lok on the steering wheel gave him an extra sense of security.

He went inside and up the stairs to the room where the singers, musicians and listeners gathered. He was glad to see that the sign on the door said: -

SINGER'S NIGHT TONIGHT

This meant that there would be no 'Guest Artiste' so anyone who got up to play would have enough time to do three or four songs. A smaller notice, at eye level, said: -

PLEASE WAIT FOR APPLAUSE BEFORE ENTERING

This was a must in acoustic clubs; it was considered bad manners to enter the room during a performance.

"Geoff! Long time no see!" said Steve as Geoff walked in to the room.

It would be at least half an hour before the music started so Geoff felt quite safe ignoring the second sign.

Carol came across and gave him a hug. "Sorry to hear about Lute" she said, "It was such a shock."

"You can say that again," said Geoff.

"What brings you to Cromwell's Cave then?" asked Steve "I know it's not the beer."

Geoff explained that he had been to Lute's funeral and then back to Jackie's for drinks.

"Poor Jackie," said Carol "She must be devastated."

"She's had a hard time since Lute got made redundant," said Geoff

"We hadn't seen either of them since Jackie had the baby, must be over four years," said Steve.

The conversation wound up as the regulars started to arrive. There were an amazing array of instruments, housed in black cases of various shapes and sizes, being carried into the room: guitars, banjos, flutes, melodeons, whistles, bodrahns and even a hurdy gurdy. Despite the fact that he was driving, and could only risk a couple of pints, Geoff knew that he was in for a good night; it was always a good night at 'The Cave'.

Pushing Forté kicked off at eight-thirty Sharp. Steve welcomed everyone to 'The Cave.' They sang *'I'm Always Glad To See a Mon Like Thee.'* And dedicated it to Geoff. He acknowledged the fact and thought, to himself, that he would probably come to this friendly club more often if it was closer to home.

Steve and Carol sang three songs, and then invited the first singer of the evening, to come to the front and perform. The chap was an acoustic blues guitarist from Blackburn, who went by the name of 'Woody'. He could really make the instrument talk.

Next was a couple from Preston; the guy played the concertina and his lady-friend played a tin whistle on their first number and sang beautifully on the next one.

Several other musicians and singers, some brilliant, some average and some who were not very good but very keen followed them. The great thing about the 'Cave' was that, whatever their level, all performers were appreciated and treated as equals.

Steve announced a short break and said that Carol would be coming around with the usual raffle, which was for the customary bottle of wine. He said that he had spoken to the treasurer and the secretary and they had agreed that tonight's proceeds would go towards Lute's benefit gig, details of which would be given to them when available.

Pushing Forté started the second half with a couple of short Scottish songs - *Leezie Lindsay* and *Bogeys Bonnie Belle.* Steve then announced: "We've a bit of a treat for you tonight, a man who has not been to the cave for some time, could you please welcome - from Elderflower Punch - Geoff!"

He stepped forwards and received a welcoming applause. "Can you do three?" asked Steve.

Geoff obliged, he removed his Dreadnought from its flight case and checked the tuning; it was fine.

"Thanks," he said to the audience, "It's nice to be here again." He sang his arrangement of Gordon Lightfoot's *In The Early Morning Rain.* The audience thoroughly enjoyed it.

Next he picked up the mandolin and explained to the audience about how he had come by it earlier that day and how Jackie had asked him to think about Lute and her and young John whenever he played it.

"I'm a novice on this thing," said Geoff "But I should be able to strum along to something simple, anyone got a request?"

He froze for a few seconds, when a female voice, that he somehow recognised, shouted from a gloomy corner, at the back of the room "HOW ABOUT THE ROSE OF THE RIBBLE VALLEY?"

He stared at the girl who made the request and although she was semi-silhouetted, due to the spotlight that illuminated the performers, Geoff was pretty sure he knew who she was. He didn't know her name though because last time he had met her she had fled before he had managed to formally introduce himself.

She was the girl in his dream.

Never being one to refuse a challenge, especially one thrown down by an attractive female, Geoff had a go at the song. Considering that he had only acquired the mandolin a few hours before and had only sung the song in a dream, he did very well. He kept to a simple strum pattern and used a basic three-chord trick. Because the neck of the mandolin was tiny, in comparison with his guitar, he had to keep an eye on where he was placing his fingers. He managed to sing the five verses without tripping over the words. As he finished the fifth verse he looked across at the girl hoping that maybe she would carry on and sing the extra verse that she had sung so beautifully in his dream. She didn't, he couldn't see her, she had disappeared. He ended the song quite abruptly.

The audience gave it their vote and the enthusiastic applause should have pleased Geoff but his mind was elsewhere "Thank you very much ladies and gentlemen, that was a Brian Clayton composition." he said as he picked up his instruments and walked back to his seat.

There was a pause in the normally flawless proceedings.

Steve jumped to his feet and went to the front to introduce the next singer "Thank you Geoff." He said. The audience clapped again. "And please don't leave it so long next time."

As Steve was returning to his seat, next to Carol, he stopped at Geoff's table, "Sorry mate!" he said, "I thought you were doing three?"

"It seemed right to finish after that one," said Geoff.

Steve thought that Geoff looked somewhat 'distant' and thought maybe it was due to the funeral and playing Lute's mandolin. "You OK mate?"

"I'm fine," said Geoff "It's been a strange sort of a day."

As was tradition, at the end of the evening, a number of Cave regulars, got up to form an impromptu band. They sang a couple of 'rip-roarers' that everyone joined in with, and then, as always, finished off with an unaccompanied version of *The Wild Mountain Thyme*.

The bar had closed some thirty minutes earlier so most people had finished their drinks and headed home as soon as the last song had finished. Geoff hung around while Carol sorted out the raffle money and Steve offered the services of 'Pushing Forté' for the, as yet unplanned, benefit night.

Carol handed Geoff twenty-seven pounds to go towards Lute's fund. "That's about double our normal take," she said. "Most of our regulars remembered him when he used to play here."

Geoff bade them both goodnight and made his way downstairs and out onto the almost empty car park. He opened the boot and placed the instruments inside; a sixth sense, accompanied by an awareness of a strong smell of roses, told him that someone was behind him. He turned around quickly.

It was the flaxen haired beauty from his dream but gone was the plain brown sackcloth frock, now she was wearing jeans and a pink woollen jumper and around her neck was the pewter rose pendant, still hanging on the leather thong.

"Sorry did I startle you?" she smiled "It's Geoff isn't it?"

He nodded politely.

She went on. "I'm Rosemary, but you can call me Rose."

Chapter 9

A Rose by any other name.

To say that Geoff was confused, by the sudden appearance of this beautiful young lady, would have been an understatement. He wanted to reach out and touch her, to see if she was real, but had no wish to offend or frighten her, which may cause her to flee like she had done in the dream. His instincts told him that he needed to handle this situation with care.

"Well hello Rose, " he said, "it's so nice to see you again, maybe this time we can talk a little."

"That would indeed be a pleasure, though a lady must be wary of your charm if you converse as sweetly as you sing." She replied in a manner of speaking that was from an age long gone.

"I don't know about 'charm,'" said Geoff smiling "But I do know that it's dark out here and getting cold. Would you like a lift home?"

"A lift?" she replied inquisitively "I live about eight miles eastward, it would be far to much to expect a gentleman to carry me over that distance."

"Actually I was thinking of driving you!" He said, with a smile, slapping his hand on the roof of the car.

"This is your carriage?"

"It gets me from A to B." Said Geoff.

"How could a lady turn down such a chivalrous offer?"

She held out her hand to him as he opened the car door; not as a token of affection though, she was looking to be helped into the 'carriage'. Geoff touched her hand, she was real enough all right.

He got in and started up the engine, pulled out of the car park and onto the road. "Where am I taking you?" he asked.

"Stay on the main Clitheroe highway and I will tell you when we are there."

Geoff assumed that she meant the A59 but had a strange feeling that it would be pointless to discuss road numbers with the girl. He took the B road through Cuerden to join the A59 at Samlesbury. 'As the crow flies' it was the straightest route.

"What do you want with me?" asked Geoff. She didn't answer, she just stirred out of the window oblivious to everything. "This is going to be a great conversation" he thought, maybe she was falling asleep.

He turned on the car's stereo cassette player; it was John Denver singing *Leaving on a Jet Plane*. The girl turned to look at him; it was if she was not aware of any music playing.

"In answer to your question," she said, "I want nothing of you, I only seek the minstrel."

"Where do I come into this then?" Asked Geoff, "This is the second time our paths have crossed and both times you seemed to have an interest in me."

"You sing his song! Badly I may add, but nevertheless you sing it."

"Thanks for the compliment, it's encouraging." Said Geoff. "Anyway it's Brian's song, he's a friend of mine and he wrote it!"

"That's true Bryan of Clayton composed it, for me. He is my minstrel."

"You mean Brian Clayton the folk-singer."

" I only know him as 'Bryan of Clayton' the sweetest singing minstrel in the Ribble Valley and by far the most handsome man in the county."

Geoff was confused he was quite certain that they were not talking about the same man.

"Tell me about your minstrel," said Geoff "Where does he live? What does he look like?"

"He travels between Clitheroe and Preston playing the halls and the castles, he truly is a wandering minstrel. When his travels take him past my cot he stays with me."

"Are you lovers?"

"We were betrothed but it is now not to be. I am, through no fault of my own, with child by another and those wretched

Croxleighs are preventing me from contacting my beloved Bryan. I fear that they have imprisoned him or worse."

"Have you reported this to the authorities?" asked Geoff.

"Croxleigh is the Lord of the Manor, he is the authority, it would do me no good to relate my tale of woe to him. The child, which is now in my belly, came about when Croxleigh's son took me without my consent."

"You mean Stan Croxley raped you?"

"I know nothing of a Stan Croxleigh," said Rose " It was Gerald, the youngest son, who did the deed."

The conversation was beginning to get very heavy, maybe the girl was a 'schizo' or under the influence of some substance or other.

"What about the song?" said Geoff "Did you say that Brian composed it for you?"

"Yes he composed the ditty for me and first sang it on the day I accepted his proposal of marriage; he sang it so sweetly, I fear he will never sing it again."

"How many verses were there?" asked Geoff "Five or six?"

"Although he wrote a sixth verse for me, I only ever heard him sing the five!"

"But you sang the sixth verse in the dream!"

The girl changed the subject, "My cot lies in yonder wood and it would please me to alight at the gates."

Geoff looked out and saw the wall that skirted Croxley's Wood on his right-hand side. He saw the gate in the distance and slowed down. He pulled up on the grass verge adjacent to the large double gates.

"You're telling me that you live in there?" Said Geoff, pointing to the wood. "We're in the middle of nowhere and those gates haven't been opened for God knows how long."

"The path through the trees leads to the hall where I live," she said "Now could you please open the carriage door and let me out? The track will be far too narrow for your horses to turn around."

Geoff thought he should try and humour her. "I can leave the horses and carriage here and escort you, on foot, if you wish." He said as he helped her out of the passenger door.

"That will not be necessary and it certainly would not be proper, I hardly know you."

She walked towards the gate and pushed it open. "Maybe our paths will cross again Geoff, goodnight!" The air filled with the smell of roses at it wafted out from the wood.

She closed the gate behind her.

A sudden urge came upon Geoff; he had to follow her. He pushed the gate to open it; it wouldn't budge an inch. Even in the moonlight he could see the large lock fastened securely on the rusty asp and staple. The ivy clinging tightly to the wood suggested that these gates had not moved for many years.

Chapter 10

Into The Lirium.

Geoff walked across the soft earth of the verge, wiped his feet on the grass and got back into his car. He couldn't make any sense whatsoever about what had just taken place, either the strange conversation with the girl or what had happened when he tried to open the gate.

He started up and moved the wheel to pull out onto the road and almost jumped out of his skin when the loud air horn of an approaching lorry sounded, warning him of its presence. His mind was in such turmoil that he had not been concentrating on the road. He held up his hand as an apology and an admission of guilt. The lorry driver flashed his lights in acknowledgement. Looking through his rear-view mirror Geoff watched the lorry disappear into the distance, the red rose of 'Ribble Valley Electrics' getting smaller and smaller.

He couldn't sleep he kept going over the strange chain of events over and over again. He was very sceptical about things supernatural and certainly didn't believe in ghosts even though just up the road, at Samlesbury Hall, people regularly encountered the famous White Lady.

He got out of bed at ten-thirty, after a very restless night, and made himself toast and a strong cup of coffee. He had to go back and have a close look at the gates in daylight. It was a Friday morning, he was supposed to be at work, he phoned in and booked a day holiday.

He parked up in a lay-by on the opposite side of the road, about three hundred and fifty yards away from the gates. He crossed the road and walked along the verge that was permanently in the shadow of the overhanging foliage of Croxley's wood.

Geoff cursed to himself as he walked along the verge and arrived at the gate, his trainers were getting heavy due to the muddy, peaty like earth that was sticking to them. He had already spent almost half an hour or so cleaning his best shoes, which he had worn the previous evening. Looking down at his feet, he noticed the tyre tracks where he had parked his car, on the verge, the previous evening. Marking a trail, over the twenty feet, or so, between the tyre tracks and the gate was a line of footprints, well defined, in the soft ground. Geoff noticed that the prints were all identical and obviously made by one person. They were his prints. There was no sign whatsoever of any smaller prints, that should have been left by the girl.

He re-examined the gates, this time in the full light of day. There was no evidence of them recently being opened. He wasn't imagining last night's events; the girl was real alright, he'd touched her and seen her push the gate open and go through. There must be a logical explanation and it could probably be found on the other side of the gates. He decided to climb over and look around.

He grabbed the top of the gates and pulled himself up. He found a foothold on top of the lock, which allowed him to cock his other leg over the top of the gates and sit himself straddled with one leg on either side of the wooden barrier. A section of rotten wood came away in his hand. Luckily the gate that was taking his weight was solid unlike its partner, the top end of which was obviously rotten.

Although he had driven past Croxley's Wood on many occasions, this was the first time that he had ever had a chance to look inside. It was an extremely dense wood with holly and bramble filling in any gaps, making any access between the trunks of the trees impossible. The area, below him, on the 'wood' side of the gates, however, was not as dense and although the ground was covered in bracken there was an obvious vestige of a track, about ten feet wide that was inviting him to climb down and go further into the wood.

He held on to the top of the solid gate and lowered himself onto the bracken-covered ground below. As soon as his feet touched the floor he became aware of the heavy scent of roses.

He made his way up a slope, along the undisturbed bracken-covered track. About seventy-five yards into the wood he came upon a relatively large clearing, which formed a woodland glade. Geoff was suddenly overcome with a weird sensation of *deja vous*. He knew this place; it was the same woodland glade that he had visited in his dream. He walked over towards the log on which he had sat whilst playing and singing the song. The rose bushes that had been in full bloom, all around the clearing, during his vision, were not yet in flower; however there was a single pink rose that had been deliberately placed on top of the log. Geoff looked at the bloom, adjacent to it, newly scratched into the thin bark on the log was a message, it said "Please help find us, we are lost!"

Geoff picked up the rose and put it in his pocket. He made his way back across the clearing, the bracken came up to his knees and he was taking high steps to avoid tripping over it. As he put his foot down he stepped on something solid, it suddenly lifted from out of the bracken, in a pivoting motion and struck him hard on the shinbone. He examined the object; it was a robust plastic box about six inches high and two feet square. The lid was made from a fine plastic mesh and inside were sheets of what looked like blotting paper. Looking around, Geoff realised that there were dozens of these contraptions in the bracken, around the edge of the clearing. He had no idea what purpose they served.

He made his way back towards the gates, it wasn't fear that was compelling him to do this; his instinct was telling him that the woods would reveal no more clues to the recent chain of events. He climbed back over the gates, returned to his car and drove home.

He placed the rose in the wineglass on top of the TV set, alongside the, now dried-up, bloom that had appeared on the pillow after his dream.

He picked up the phone and dialled Chloe.

"Hi Chloe, it's Geoff. Are you still involved with the dig on Croxley's land?"

"Hi Geoff! We've actually done as much digging as we can, we're now tidying up the loose ends."

"Did you find anything interesting?"

"We didn't make any 'earth shattering' discoveries, if that's what you mean," said Chloe, "I think there maybe some interesting stuff under what is now the bowling greens but Croxley wouldn't give us permission to dig there."

"How are you on Croxley history?" asked Geoff.

"I'm more interested in what went on prior to the Croxley or Croxleigh involvement," said Chloe "What do you want to know?"

"Chloe, this is embarrassing for me, I'm a very sceptical person but I need to talk to someone. I think I may have seen a ghost!"

Chapter 11

Chloe pays a visit.

Chloe turned up at quarter to nine that evening. She had asked Geoff to write down as much as he could remember, preferably in chronological order, so that she would have some sort of manageable structure to enable her to begin her investigation.

Geoff told her about the dream and the meeting at Cromwell's Cave, including the lift home. He told her about the girl's references to Bryan of Clayton and the Croxleys, the sixth verse to the song and the mysterious roses.

He took a break for drinks, "Fruit juice I suppose?" he said to Chloe.

"Maybe something a little stronger," she said. "Have you any wine?"

Geoff was a beer man through and through he never drank wine. "Sorry Chloe, it's either beer or whisky?"

"I'll have a whisky and lemonade please?"

He poured a can of bitter into a pint pot for himself and put some whisky and lemonade into a small glass tumbler for Chloe.

They settled down and got back to grips with Geoff's account of things.

"Can you remember anything else that might be relevant?" asked Chloe.

Geoff thought hard, "Roses!" he said, "A strong smell of roses both in the dream and during my subsequent meeting with her at Cromwell's Cave and then again in Croxley's Wood."

That's interesting," said Chloe, "I'm no expert in these matters but I do recall reading somewhere that strong sweet smells often precede paranormal experiences."

"But I first smelt it at Brian's cottage," said Geoff, "He did something weird with the drinks."

"When was this?" Asked Chloe.

"On the same night that I had the dream, I'd spent the evening with Brian and Tina."

"Tell me what he did with the drinks." She said.

Geoff looked at the roses on top of the TV. "I don't need to tell you," he said, "I can show you."

He took the dried rose from the glass and tore up and crushed the petals and put them in a neat pile on the coffee table. Next he poured two cans of best bitter into a plastic measuring-jug and stirred in the crushed petals. The red-hot poker would be a problem. Geoff used a gas fire to heat his room, however there was a small poker, accompanied by a brush, shovel and coal tongues, on the ornamental brass fireside companion set that was on the hearth. Geoff took the poker into the kitchen and placed the iron 'business end' over the largest ring, on the stove and ignited the gas.

Within about five minutes the poker was glowing red, he carefully carried it back into the parlour and plunged the end into the beer. There was a, now familiar hissing sound as steam rose up from the jug and with it the strong smell of roses filled the room.

Both Geoff and Chloe where overcome with a strange sense of well being, even before they sampled a drink from the jug. Geoff poured some of the contents of the jug into two half-pint glasses and handed one to Chloe; it would be interesting to see her reaction, she normally avoided alcoholic drinks.

Chloe tried a mouthful of the brew and licked the foam from her lips. "Very nice!" she said giggling, "I think it's what you call 'Mulled beer'."

"It certainly adds to the flavour," said Geoff, "It even made that cheap-nasty stuff, that Brian buys, acceptable."

"Brian Clayton!" said Chloe, "I never actually saw him play but I'm told that he was brilliant."

"He certainly was," said Geoff, "I can't understand why he ever stopped performing - he used to pack them in wherever he played."

"Maybe his wife's got him on a short leash," she said with a grin, "Probably can't cope with the adulation he got from the ladies in the audience."

Geoff laughed, "This is Folk-singing we're talking about, not rock and roll, we don't get women throwing their knickers onto the stage you know."

"I know that," she said rather coyly, "But ladies are attracted to men who play guitars. Well I am anyway."

Geoff was quite taken aback by this statement, he'd known Chloe for a couple of years now and couldn't ever remember her discussing who she 'fancied'.

He picked up the jug "Would you like another?" he asked.

"Just a small one please, it goes right through me. How about playing that Brian Clayton album? I'll pay a call while you find it."

Geoff pointed her in the direction of the bathroom.

He flipped through his album collection: Cat Stevens, John Denver, Bob Dylan, Ralph McTell, until he came upon the one with Brian's picture on the front. He carefully extracted the vinyl disc from the sleeve and placed it, carefully, onto the turntable.

It was halfway through track two when Chloe returned from the bathroom, she settled down in the armchair and picked up her drink. "No wonder he used to play to packed audiences, he's brilliant, she said as track four came to an end.

"This is the one!" said Geoff, as track five started, "The Rose of the Ribble Valley."

Chloe sat there spellbound, she closed her eyes and gently rocked her head to the music, smiling as she listened to Brian's mellow voice and arpeggio guitar.

Geoff took his guitar off the stand and strummed quietly along with the record. As Brian's voice tapered off, at the end of the recording, Geoff continued to strum the chord pattern. He couldn't quite believe what happened next.

Chloe, eyes still closed with a trance like smile on her face, sang the sixth verse, word for word, just like Rose had done it in his dream.

As Chloe stopped singing, Geoff strummed a final chord to finish the duet. "That was bloody marvelous!" he said, "Where did you find it?"

"Find what?" replied Chloe in a bewildered tone.

"The sixth verse of course!"

"What sixth verse?"

"The one you just sang!"

"I'm sorry Geoff, I'm not with you," she said, "I don't know what your going on about."

"Chloe you just sang the missing verse, when the record finished you carried on!"

"I don't remember anything at all, it must be the alcohol." She looked at the beer glass in her hand and started to push herself up out of the armchair.

"Chloe!" said Geoff "Stay where you are, I'll play it again and see what happens. Sit back and close your eyes"

He dropped the stylus into the groove at the start of the track. Brian's voice and guitar came through the speakers. Geoff picked up the Martin and strummed along.

He deliberately carried on playing after the record finished. The only reaction from Chloe was that she hummed the melody without actually singing any words.

"Well that was a waste of time!" said Geoff.

"Are you sure it's not just your imagination?" said Chloe

"Positive," said Geoff "The thing is, I've heard it sung twice now and I can't remember a damned word of it."

"It's only a song," said Chloe.

"I know it as a love song with a happy ending" said Geoff "But the new verse changes all that and turns it into something sad but sinister."

"It's getting late." Chloe said.

Geoff looked at his watch. It was past midnight. He thought about Chloe and the Alcohol.

"Would you like to leave your car here and I'll phone for a taxi?"

Chloe stood up and kicked off her shoes, "You don't think that I'm going to leave you here alone with all these ghostly goings on, do you?"

She slipped her loose fitting, long, dark brown dress off her shoulders and let it slide down to the floor. She was completely naked.

Geoff was shocked but as he gazed at her he couldn't help thinking how stunningly beautiful plain old Chloe was now he was seeing her in the flesh. She reached for his hand and led him to the stairs.

"And besides, if this fragrant young lady turns up in your dreams tonight, I want to meet her." She said.

Geoff woke up, the sun was shining in through the window, he looked at the clock; it was ten-thirty on Saturday morning. He reached over to his left to caress Chloe but she wasn't there. He couldn't recall any contact with, or dreams about, Rose during the night but he had a very vivid recollection of the unadulterated, lustful, passionate lovemaking with Chloe.

Chloe pushed open the bedroom door and walked in wearing one of Geoff's shirts. She had a towel wrapped turban like around her hair. She was carrying a tray with two mugs of tea and four rounds of buttered toast.

"Thought you might fancy breakfast in bed," she said, as she rolled back the covers and got back in bed.

Geoff put his arm around her, she moved it away and handed him a mug of tea.

"Geoff, last night was the best sex I've had for ages but that's all it was, I don't want any commitments or long term relationships or any of that shit and I hope you'll accept it for what it was, just a bit of harmless fun, a one off."

"Chloe, you're wonderful!" said Geoff and he put the mug down on the bedside cabinet.

"Do you really think so?" said Chloe as she pulled off the shirt and straddled him with both legs.

"Yes" he said "Absolutely marvelous."

"I suppose there's no harm in once more for the road then," she said as she bent forward to kiss his lips.

Half an hour later, Chloe jumped out of bed and got dressed, "Saturday afternoon's reserved for taking mother round the shops," said Chloe.

"Does she know where you are?" asked Geoff, concerned.

"I used your phone this morning, before I had a shower; she thinks I spent the night at the university, it's best not to tell her too much."

Geoff got up and slipped on his dressing gown. "I'll see you at the next gig then," he said as he followed her down the stairs.

"Yes, and meanwhile I'll do some digging at the record offices at Preston and Clitheroe and see if I can find out anything about Bryan of Clayton, Rosemary and Gerald Croxleigh. I'll give the record office at Whalley Abbey a try too."

"I suppose I'd better get on with arranging the benefit concert for Lute" said Geoff.

He opened the door and leaned over to kiss her, she pulled away; "Geoff it's like me singing the missing verse, it never happened!"

He watched plain old Chloe get into her car and drive away.

Chapter 12

A concert to organise.

Geoff had been toying with asking Brian if maybe they could use the opening night at The Grey Mare for Lute's benefit concert, after all it would guarantee a full house and demonstrate that the management of the pub (Brian and Tina) were prepared to support live music. However he had last spoken to Brian over a fortnight ago and Brian's last words were "I'll be in touch." Geoff had heard nothing from him since.

He decided to take the bull by the horns and contact Brian, he tried the phone book and directory enquiries but to no avail, the Claytons were ex-directory.

He tried to think who might have the number; he could only come up with one name, Charlie Bagwell. He looked up the number of the Super Nova Entertainment Agency and dialled.

The phone rang three times then a click indicated that he had been connected to an answering machine. "Hello this is the Super Nova Entertainment Agency, suppliers of quality acts for all your entertainment needs. Sorry our operator cannot get to the phone at the moment please leave your name and number and we will get back to you."

There was a long "bleep."

"Shit" thought Geoff, it was bad enough having to talk to Bagwell himself, without having to converse with his answering machine. "Hello Charlie, its Geoff---" before he finished the sentence, Charlie, who was obviously listening to his incoming calls snatched up the receiver.

"Well well, if it isn't the folk singing super star!" said Charlie sarcastically. "You've got a fucking nerve ringing here. I suppose you want me to get you some dates to fill in all the cancellations in your diary. Well you can fuck off!"

"Charlie!" said Geoff "I'm not out for an argument, I just needed your help, if you don't want to then that's fine with me."

Bagwell didn't want to totally sever relations with Geoff, after all Elderflower Punch where still in big demand for Free Masons functions and silver weddings and that was worth seventeen and a half per-cent of some pretty hefty fees. However he had decided that he was going to make Geoff grovel a bit for the outburst at the Malt Shovel.

"You want help from me? 'A slime ball who's killing live music' - your words not mine."

"Sorry Charlie I was having a bad time."

"You were having a bad time! What about me? I come home to find that miserable bastard mandolin player bleeding to death all over my fucking office."

"Hang about Charlie! Lute was a mate of mine."

"Bollocks, you couldn't stand the condescending little twat, you've told me that often enough in the past."

"OK Charlie, Lute and I had our differences but now he's gone I'd like to put them all to rest, if that' OK with you?"

There was a pause.

"Yeah! Sorry Geoff, it's had a bad effect on us all, what do you want?"

"Have you got Brian Clayton's phone number?"

"Geoff, Geoff, you know I can't give you that, first rule of running an agency, never give out the phone numbers of the clients or the celebs."

"You awkward bastard Bagwell!" thought Geoff.

"I don't want to book him Charlie! You don't need to worry about your commission. I need to talk to him about a benefit concert that we intend to do, to raise a few quid for Lute's son, John!"

"There's no chance of getting Brian to play again" said Bagwell "he's retired, I could guarantee him two-fifty for a Saturday Night, he's just not interested anymore."

"I know that Charlie, I just wanted to ask him if we could hold the concert at his new venue."

"Right," said Charlie " I'm with you, just a minute while I get the file."

Geoff heard the receiver go down on the desk top, he could hear a drawer opening.

"Here it is Geoff, for fuck's sake don't tell him you got it from me."

Geoff jotted the number down. "Thanks Charlie, I owe you one."

"Listen Geoff" said Charlie, "about all this business with the cancellations, I don't cancel, I'm better off putting your band out for a hundred quid, than a self contained singer for forty but that's the way the market's going. If I miss the boat I'll drown, it's as simple as that." He went on; "I've had some bloody good commissions from booking your band, if there's anything I can do to help with this concert let me know."

"Cheers Charlie," said Geoff "how would you feel about loaning us one of your sound systems for the evening?"

"Consider it done," said Bagwell "Let me know where and when."

"Thanks Charlie, I'll get back to you."

Geoff hung up then picked up the receiver again to dial Brian.

"Hello," It was Tina's voice.

"Hi Tina! It's Geoff, can I have a word with Brian?"

"Hi Geoff" said Tina "He's not in, is there anything I can do?"

Geoff couldn't help thinking that Tina sounded a bit tipsy even to the point of slurring her words.

"I was going to ask him how his pub project's going and needed to ask a favour."

"All he ever bloody thinks about is his bloody pub project, I don't get a bloody look in, I don't think he'd bloody notice if I fucked off and left him to it."

This was definitely the voice of someone under the influence, thought Geoff. He needed to handle it with care.

"Tina, be a love and ask him to give me a ring when he gets home please."

"If he gets home you mean, he's got more important things in his life than me, he doesn't give a shit about me anymore! Why don't you go down to the bowling club, you'll probably find him there."

"Thanks Tina."

Geoff had hoped to get everything sorted on the phone, he hadn't planned on driving anywhere, but needs must and the concert needed arranging; he also needed to pop into Preston for some guitar strings so he could call at Brian's pub on the way back.

The old Convent Bowling Club was down by the riverbank, on the opposite side of the main road, from Croxley's Wood. Although many of the trees had been cleared it was obvious that in days gone by, prior to the building of the dual carriageway, Croxley's Wood must have stretched all the way down to the river.

Geoff was on the dual carriageway with Croxley's Wood on his right hand side. He was slowing down ready to turn left down Monkswood Lane towards the old bowling club when something caught his eye. Ahead, in the distance there was some activity on the verge, near the gates that he had scaled the previous day. He ignored the right turn and continued along the road to have a close look. There were a couple of cars parked on the grass. Blazing away on the verge was a bonfire that Geoff presumed must have been the gates, burning. Two workmen were fitting a new pair of extremely robust, solid wooden gates into the gap.

Geoff carried on to the roundabout and turned around, as he drove back he was on the right side of the road to enable him to get a closer look. A well-dressed man got out of one of the cars and went over to the workmen. It was Stan Croxley.

Geoff carried on for another few hundred yards, indicated right and turned into Monkswood Lane. The last time he'd been down here was when he had been supporting Brian at a gig. He smiled to himself as he thought of Brian driving there and Tina driving back, he thought about his earlier phone conversation, with Tina, and wondered what had gone wrong between her and Brian.

The narrow wooded lane was about three-quarters of mile long and was a relatively steep drop down towards the river, it widened out at the end and Geoff couldn't believe what he saw.

The old timber and tin built bowling club had been replaced by a beautiful stone building and there was a sign erected on an ornate pole at the front of the building. Emblazoned on the sign was a picture of a grey horse, astride its back was an angelic minstrel playing a harp. The wording was in bold crimson and gold lettering it read: -

THE GREY MARE

Geoff parked his car at the front of the pub. He tried the front door; it was locked. There was no doorbell or knocker so he decided to try his luck round the back.

There where three other vehicles parked by the side of the pub: a Morris Traveller, a Rover and a Transit van that, judging from the sign writing, belonged to Langho Carpets. As Geoff walked down the side of the building he spotted a couple of elderly gentlemen who were locking up the hut that was next to the two magnificent bowling greens that still graced the riverbank. The air smelt of freshly cut grass and by their attire he figured that they had been mowing the greens rather than playing bowls.

"Ow'do," said one of the men, "Grand day!"

"Certainly is," said Geoff "Is there anyone about?"

"They're round t'back" said his colleague, in a broad Lancashire accent "Th'all hav'ta knock on t'window."

"Cheers." said Geoff.

As he got round the back he could hear a radio blurring out. He tried the door again, it was locked so he took the old man's advice and knocked on the window. The door opened.

"Geoff!" said Brian as he stepped outside; "You've come to see what we're up to then" he smiled with enthusiasm like a proud father wanting to show off his newborn son.

"Well I hadn't heard from you so I thought 'if the mountain won't come to Mohammed' and all that." said Geoff with a grin.

"Sorry mate I've really meant to ring you but I've been so busy here, you know what it's like and I'm still waiting for the Post Office to sort a bloody phone line out. Anyway come in, have a look, have a drink. You'll have to settle for tea though because we're a pub with no beer for at least another week or so."

Geoff laughed; he had fond memories of Brian singing *'A Pub With No Beer'* on the gigs they did together.

"I can't show you the bar just yet," said Brian "I've a couple of guys in there fitting carpets, they must be on a bonus scheme, they get really pissed off if you disturb them but come and look at the concert room."

Geoff stood back in amazement; the room was a performer's dream. There was a small stage at one end big enough for a four-piece band, with drums. There were three rows of eight seats in front of the stage, which could be moved to accommodate a screw down wooden dance floor when required.

Behind the rows of seats was a step up to another level that contained chairs and tables to seat about eighty people. There were also two upholstered bench type seats that ran all the way along the sidewalls. These would seat another twenty people, if required. The back wall had shutters, which could be opened to access the bar, these could be open when bands were amplified or kept shut for the quieter acoustic sessions.

The ceiling was covered with acoustic tiles and a small bank of suspended spotlights pointed at the stage. The windows were all covered by thick velvet curtains, which would help to maintain the sound quality in the room.

"It's great," said Geoff. "Did you plan it all yourself?"

"Kind of," said Brian, "but the sound and lighting experts like to change things around a bit. I wanted the tables and chairs on two levels, you know, higher at the back but the sound advice man talked me out of it and said that it would be better as it is now."

"Wow," said Geoff "I can't wait to play in here, when do you open?"

"Officially, a week on Saturday but I can't start the music until a week later because the sound people haven't finished building the in-house system; pity really because I would have liked to have opened with something special on the first night."

"Well how do you fancy a concert on your opening night and it won't cost you a penny."

"How am I going to do that?" asked Brian.

Geoff explained about Lute's benefit.

"That's fine with me," said Brian "what about a sound system though? Your rig's not big enough for this place."

"It's in-hand," said Geoff, "Bagwell's going to let us use one like he had over at the Shovel."

"Sorted then!" said Brian; "Let me have the line-up and I'll do some posters."

"Cheers Brian, I'll put something in the paper."

"By the way Geoff, let's get one thing clear, please don't ask me to get up and perform. The official line is that 'I've retired at my peak', but between you and me, it upsets Tina."

"I spoke to her, on the phone, this morning," said Geoff, "I got the impression that you were in the bad books."

"How did she sound?"

"To be honest Brian she sounded as if she had been hitting the bottle!"

"No it's not drink mate, it's drugs, prescribed by her shrink, anti-depressants and tranquillisers, and they have that sort of effect."

"Shrink? I didn't have Tina down as a head-case." Said Geoff.

"It's difficult to explain but it's my fault," said Brian; "Tina's jealous."

"Jealous? What of?" asked Geoff.

"Another woman!" said Brian.

"You mean you've been caught 'playing away from home'?" said Geoff, although he would never have thought it of Brian.

"Not exactly," said Brian, "I said it's a bit of a difficult one; the woman, that Tina is jealous of is some sort of ah," he paused "shall we say a figment of my imagination, I dream about her!"

"She's not called Rosemary by any chance?" asked Geoff.

Brian's jaw dropped; "How the fuck did you know that?"

"I gave her a lift home the other night!"

Chapter 13

Brian's story.

Geoff could see that Brian was physically shocked at his revelation about Rosemary.

"We need to talk about this," said Brian, "over a brew. Tea or coffee?"

"Whatever comes," said Geoff.

Brian brewed two mugs of tea and gave one to Geoff; "Come on let's sit outside and get away from the smell of paint and new carpets." He said.

They sat on an ornate bench that overlooked the bowling greens, it was a warm spring afternoon and the sun was shining.

"What made you decide to keep the bowling greens?" asked Geoff.

"They've been playing bowls here for years, Tina's dad said that as long as the old boys were prepared to look after the greens they could stay."

"That's nice of him, I suppose it guarantees you some custom at lunchtime." said Geoff.

"Yes, but I'm not going to get rich on a half of mild and ten woodbines."

They both laughed.

"Well" said Brian "it's your turn first, tell me what you know about Rose?"

Geoff told Brian his story about the dream he'd had after drinking the beer at Dunstrummin and about meeting Rose at Cromwell's Cave, driving her home and the conversation that had taken place. He told him about climbing into Croxley's Wood and the message on the log.

He also mentioned Chloe singing the sixth verse of the song after trying some beer with the rose petal treatment.

Brian scratched his head. "It's a long story," he said, "give me your pot and I'll make a refill."

Brian brought out two fresh mugs of tea.

"It all started with that bloody song." He said "The Rose of the Ribble Valley"

"You didn't write it did you?" said Geoff.

"I never claimed to have done," said Brian "it's just an assumption incorrectly made by a lot of people. Look at the credit on the album sleeve, it's Bryan with a 'Y'."

"Bryan of Clayton?" asked Geoff.

"Yes"

"Did Rose give you the song?"

"No! Rose didn't turn up until after we were married; I'd recorded the album a couple of years earlier."

"How did you come across it then?"

"Actually it seems a bit ironic now; Tina gave it me. When her grandmother, on her dad's side, died, she found it when the family was sorting out the old lady's stuff. It was on a parchment neatly pressed inside the back pages of her grandmother's bible. Obviously when it said Bryan of Clayton on it Tina showed it to me."

"Have you still got it? The parchment I mean not the bible."

"No! Tina's dad, Frank Croxley, took it away and locked it up with all the other family paraphernalia, the Croxley's like to keep their family history very private; it's something they don't discuss even with their son-in-law, never mind outsiders."

"How many verses were there?"

"Definitely only the five; you're the only person who has mentioned a sixth verse. Although come to think of it, each time I've met Rose, and as I said that's only in my dreams, she uses her expert powers of persuasion to try and make me sing the song and then always looks and acts disappointed when I've finished."

"You mean Tina's jealous of a dream?"

"Yes, it's embarrassing but apparently I give a running commentary all the way through and go into every little detail."

"Can you not just turn over and do the business with Tina."

"No that's just it Geoff, Tina can't cope with the fact that it's a dream or a haunting or whatever you want to call it. You say you've met her, then you know she's more than just a dream."

"I've touched her Brian, or at least I think I have, she's gorgeous!"

"And then there's the flowers," said Brian, "each time I have had one of these experiences I've woken up to find a pink rose on my pillow."

"I've had those too," said Geoff, "one on the pillow and one next to the message on the log." He went on; "Has she only appeared in your dreams or have you seen her in the flesh?"

"Kind of!" said Brian, "but I can't be sure. At the last two or three gigs that I played, someone in the audience left me flowers, always a bunch of pink roses. Each time the roses were accompanied by a note reading,

' To my darling Bryan from your own Rose of the Ribble Valley'.

I don't recall actually seeing anyone; it's difficult with the stage lights, but obviously Tina got uptight about it and reckons that a girl fitting Rosemary's description was sitting, alone, in the audience. I always assumed that it was some over-enthusiastic groupie."

"So this was going on before you got married then."

"Well yes, and I think Tina felt threatened by this woman who was leaving me bunches of flowers; that was one of the reasons that I promised to stop playing after the wedding but I never actually dreamt about Rose until after Tina and I were married and I'd stopped performing."

"Who is Bryan of Clayton?" asked Geoff.

"I don't know," said Brian, "except that I think he may be a skeleton in the Croxley family cupboard, I broached the subject once at a family dinner party, talk about a conversation killer, Tina's old man couldn't change the subject fast enough."

"Interesting" said Geoff.

"So! What do you reckon?" asked Brian.

Geoff paused for a moment as though deep in thought; he finished his mug of tea before answering.

"I think this girl or lady, Rosemary, or whatever you want to call her is the spirit of someone long dead. She can't rest until she finds the answer to a question. Bryan of Clayton, whoever he is, has, or is, the answer, or at least part of it; she's in some sort of spectral time warp and thinks you're Bryan of Clayton, but you're not coming up with the goods."

"Jesus Geoff, you've been giving this some serious thought haven't you?"

"I'm hoping to find out more shortly, Chloe, who sings with the band, is a local historian, she's studying at Lancaster Uni. You may have seen her, she was doing some digging down here a couple of weeks ago."

"That's right," said Brian "There were a bunch of archaeologists down here, all these stones that we used to build the pub were apparently once part of a monastery that was built on this sight. The archaeologists were quite excited about it, they wanted to dig up the bowling greens but Frank wouldn't let them."

"She's going to do some more digging Brian but this time she's digging through the historical records of the area; I think the Croxley's are going to be involved somewhere along the line. Does that bother you? If it does I'll call her off."

"Geoff I want to get to the bottom of this just as much as you do, I have a lot of affection for Rose but I can't have a ghost ruining my marriage. If Chloe discovers anything I'd love to know."

Chapter 14

Discussion and a practice.

Sunday evening, Geoff phoned Wayne and Chloe to confirm the date of the benefit concert with them. It was to be a week on Saturday at The Opening Night of The Grey Mare. He knew that they would both be free because they had an agreement that worked well; they would let him know any dates that they couldn't do, well in advance, so that he could put them in his diary. This allowed him, in case of enquiries, to give any potential bookers of Elderflower Punch an instant answer, on the availability of the band. Chloe suggested that, as they did not have a gig before Lute's concert; they should get together and talk about 'just what songs they were going to play'.

Some of the numbers would be sadly lacking without Lute's mandolin.

They decided to meet up early at Cromwell's Cave on the Thursday night, have a quick chat about the play-list and then run through one or two of them in front of the audience at the folk club.

Chloe arranged to pick up Geoff at Seven. As she pulled up, outside the end-terraced house, she could see Geoff at the window, ready and waiting. She wondered whether or not his attitude towards her would have changed after the episode on the previous Friday night.

He locked the door of the house and went around the back of Chloe's car and put his guitar in the boot. He climbed into the passenger seat.

"Are you OK?" he asked.

"In what respect?" she replied with an inquiring look.

"OK" said Geoff "I know! It never happened."

"I'm sure I don't know what you're talking about." she said with a broad smile as she pulled away.

"Did you manage to find out anything?" said Geoff.

"I'm going along to Whalley Abbey on Monday to see if they have anything about the Monastery and a friend of mine, Jim, who's on my course and very good with public records, has been looking at the record offices for me, he should have something by tomorrow."

They drove past the entrance into Croxley's Wood; Geoff explained about the new gates. A black circle of charcoal on the verge was all that remained of the old pair.

"Stan Croxley was overseeing that little lot on Saturday afternoon," said Geoff.

"Do you think it's more than a coincidence?" asked Chloe.

"I'm not sure," said Geoff, "I don't want to start sounding paranoid but after you left on Saturday, I went down to the Bowling Club and had a very interesting conversation with Brian Clayton."

Geoff filled Chloe in the details of his chat with Brian.

"He suspects skeletons in the Croxley family cupboard." said Geoff

"From what Jim says it will have to be a very big cupboard indeed." said Chloe as she pulled onto the car park of the workingmen's club

"Looks like we're not the first here." said Geoff, pointing to Wayne's van over in the corner. "Let's hope he's got the beer in."

They walked into the games-room and sure enough Wayne was sitting there with two pints and an orange juice. "It's about bloody time!" he said smiling. It was ten minutes past seven; they had arranged to meet at a quarter past.

Geoff joked, "You're keen mate! Is it happy hour?"

Wayne smiled at Chloe "That's all he cares about you know, the price of a bloody pint."

They all laughed.

"Right," said Geoff "down to business, everything's set for a week on Saturday. We'll play as a trio, Steve and Carol are going to do the Pushing Forté bit and Wayne's had a word with Woody who's a great acoustic blues Guitarist. We'll sort the running orders out nearer the time"

"What about collecting the tickets on the door and that sort of thing?" asked Chloe?

"I just thought we'd have a two quid charge on the door, why go to the expense of having tickets printed?" said Geoff.

"No problem, Dave and Julie Jackson said that they would collect the door money and help sell the raffle tickets."

"That's a bloody good idea," said Wayne "If Julie flashes her cleavage at the punters she'll sell double."

Geoff laughed

Chloe tried not to but had to submit to a giggle and a smile as she said, "Julie is rather well-blessed in that department."

"I went into the Brown Cow yesterday to pick up a microphone stand," said Wayne "Dougie gave me twenty quid to put towards the total, he's also said that we can offer Sunday lunch for two as a raffle prize."

"What about publicity?" asked Chloe?

"Brian's doing some posters and I've spoken to The Post and The Telegraph, they are both going to do a couple of paragraphs," said Geoff; "I've also written to Radio Lancashire."

"We can plug it here tonight," said Chloe "I'll pop into the Pig and Whistle on Tuesday and let them know about it and Dave and Julie said they'll mention it at Clitheroe Folk Club tomorrow.

Geoff was quite happy with the arrangements and was confident that the night would be well supported by local music fans, as was always the case on this sort of occasion.

Steve and Carol arrived at about ten minutes past eight; Steve spotted Geoff and Co. when he came into the bar for the key to the upstairs room. "Well this is an honour!" he said to Geoff, "two weeks running and this time you've brought the band."

"It's a bit of a commercial break," said Chloe, "we've come along to plug Lute's benefit concert a week on Saturday."

"You're more than welcome said Carol you can plug it as much as you want. Steve and I feel privileged that you've asked us to come along and support you on the evening."

"We appreciate you coming," said Wayne, the whole idea is to provide an evening of good quality musical entertainment and you and Steve certainly fit the bill."

"Flattery will get you everywhere!" said Carol giving Wayne an exaggerated wink.

Steve, pretending to be shocked by the reply, said to Wayne "If you can afford the shopping bills you can take her."

The five of them burst into fits of laughter and made their way upstairs.

Carol took some flyers out of her handbag, "Maybe you should sign me up as your publicity agent," she said. She showed one to Geoff, it read: -

BENEFIT CONCERT

In memory of John 'Lute' Luther
With
Elderflower Punch
Pushing Forté
& Woody
An evening of Folk & Fun
The Grey Mare
Monkswood Lane.
8:00 Saturday…

"That's marvellous," said Geoff, "why didn't I think of that?"

"I ran them off on the Xerox machine at work," said Carol; "I did plenty so if anyone's going to the Pig on Tuesday they can take some along."

"I'm going," said Chloe, "Remind me to pick them up on the way out."

Carol placed a couple of the flyers on each tabletop. Steve arranged the chairs so that no one would be sitting with their back to the stage. Unlike the week before, which was a 'Singers Night,' tonight Cromwell's Cave Folk Club had booked a guest so there was a one-pound entry fee that would go towards covering the artist's fee.

Mary Jones from Fleetwood was providing the entertainment tonight; not only was she a very good singer/songwriter she also performed excellent cover versions of songs by Joan Baez, Sandy Denny and Joni Mitchell as well as telling some humorous stories in between. She turned up just before the regular audience started to arrive. As soon as she walked in she acknowledged Wayne; he had played the bass guitar on her album, *Now That The Trawlers Are Gone,* which was available on cassette.

Steve had a quick word with her to explain the situation about Lute's Benefit Concert and asked if she minded Elderflower Punch singing three or four at the beginning of the second half.

"That would be great," said Mary, "I've never actually seen you play together, as a band, although I saw Geoff at Fleetwood Folk Club last year and he was very good indeed."

Pushing Forté started the evening with three songs, and then Steve introduced Mary Jones. She was an extremely competent and very entertaining performer, Geoff, Wayne and Chloe enjoyed sitting back and listening to someone else for a change.

During the Interval Steve plugged the forthcoming benefit gig and told the audience that he had a bit of a treat for them, he introduced Elderflower Punch and asked them to do three songs. Wayne opted to borrow Steve's Yamaha guitar, he hadn't brought his electric bass because it The Cave was an acoustic venue with no amplification.

They started off with Geoff doing the lead vocal on *Carrickfergus,* followed by *Maid's When You're Young,* with Chloe taking the lead and making the audience squeal with laughter. Geoff thanked Pushing Forté for letting them do the short spot and gave everyone another reminder about Lute's concert and then went into *Early Morning Rain.* The audience shouted for "more!" Geoff looked across at Steve who in turn looked at Mary (it would be considered bad manners to go straight into an encore on a 'Guest evening' unless you were actually the guest).

Mary smiled and gave a nod of approval.

Chloe asked the audience if there was anything in particular that they would like to hear. A female voice from the back shouted "Hey Geoff! Do that Brian Clayton song that you did last week."

Before Geoff had time to answer Chloe said, "I think we can manage that!"

Geoff gave her a puzzled look.

Wayne said "What key?"

"G Major!" said Geoff

Geoff strummed the chords and sang the verses, Chloe harmonised as Wayne weaved in and out between the chords and the lyrics with a wonderful vibrato style pick. This was the first time that they had played the song together as a band and Geoff had to really concentrate on what he was doing; however he couldn't help glancing over to where the request had come from, in the hope of seeing a flaxen haired beauty. No such luck.

Judging by the applause, the song had gone down very well with the audience. A couple approached from the back of the room, Geoff assumed that it was the lady who had requested the song.

"Thank you very much, that was lovely," she said "Unfortunately we can't make it to the concert but please put this in the pot." Her partner handed Geoff a crisp five-pound note.

"It will go to a good home!" said Geoff smiling at the couple.

Mary Jones was waiting to take the stage and Geoff was conscious of holding her up; after all she was the guest for the evening. He smiled apologetically at her and picked up his guitar in one hand and the case in the other and went to the back of the room to join Chloe and Wayne. As always his priority was to put the Martin away safely; he opened the case, he had to look twice, Chloe had seen them too. There were two large fragrant pink roses inside.

Chapter 15

Meet Jim.

Mary Jones finished her set. Steve shook her hand and thanked her then, as tradition dictated, he asked the audience if they would like another. The loud applause and standing ovation suggested that they did.

Wayne was besotted with Mary's performance, he was a connoisseur of fine musicianship and Mary played and sang extremely well indeed. Wayne was so preoccupied with watching Mary, he hadn't even noticed that Chloe and Geoff had left the room; they had far more important things on their minds than to worry about watching Mary.

"Don't take the piss Geoff," said Chloe.

They were sat at a table downstairs in the relative quiet of the clubs games room.

"If you put those roses in there to frighten me, well I don't think it's funny"

"Chloe," said Geoff "I'm telling you they weren't there when I took my guitar out of the case, and I certainly didn't put them there, honestly, you've got to believe me."

"Well who the hell put them there?" said Chloe, "And why two of them this time?"

"I think it was Rosemary," said Geoff "I think it's one rose for me plus an extra one for you. I think she wants us to help her."

"We'll talk about it on the way home, come on let's go back upstairs." said Chloe.

They got back just in time to hear Mary's encore. She sang Joni Mitchell's *Big Yellow Taxi,* everyone in the audience joined in.

Chloe and Geoff said their goodbyes and left Wayne in discussing music with Mary, Steve and Carol.

Geoff couldn't help glancing around the car park in case Rosemary showed up again.

"Wishful thinking?" asked Chloe.

"I was kind of half expecting her to put in an appearance." Said Geoff.

"Even when I'm here to look after you?"

"Oh yes!" said Geoff sarcastically, "I thought it never happened."

"You'd better believe it," said Chloe, "it's certainly not going to happen tonight, I've a busy morning tomorrow, delving into the mystery of Rosemary and Bryan of Clayton."

Chloe pulled off the car park and turned onto the main road.

"I thought you were going to Whalley on Monday?" said Geoff.

I was," said Chloe, "but it's getting personal now and I want to get to the bottom of it so I'm going in the morning. Hopefully Jim will have come up with something at the record offices, so, with a bit of luck, by lunchtime, we should have something to go on."

"Is there anything else that I can do?" asked Geoff.

You can try and remember any little details, that you may have forgotten to tell me and write them down."

She went on; "If Jim's agreeable how do you fancy coming round to my place tomorrow afternoon then we can start to put everything we have together and attempt to make some make some sense out of it?"

"That's fine by me." Said Geoff "Should I bring Brian? He said he'd like to know if you discovered anything."

"I don't know whether that would be a good idea, at this point in time," said Chloe, "It maybe wiser to get all our facts right before we involve Brian; after all the records may turn up some truths about his wife's family that he'd rather not know."

"OK!" said Geoff "I can see where you're coming from."

The car pulled up outside the end-terraced house; it was five minutes before midnight.

"Fancy a night-cap?" said Geoff

"No thanks Geoff, I've really got a lot to do tomorrow, but I'd like to take one of those roses along with me."

"No problem!" Said Geoff, "Take one." He took one of the blooms from his guitar case and handed it to Chloe. "I'll see you tomorrow afternoon then, is one thirty OK?"

"That's fine!" aid Chloe.

Geoff's normal working week, of four and a half days finished at lunchtime on Fridays. He clocked off at one, on the dot, and made his way round to Chloe's house. Chloe answered the doorbell and invited him in; she asked him if he would like a cup of tea. Mrs Walmsley said that she would put the kettle on and came back five minutes later with a pot of tea and a plate full of cheese and tomato sandwiches.

"Chloe told me you were coming straight from work I thought a lad of your age would want something to eat," said Mrs Walmsley, "can't be skipping your dinner."

Geoff smiled and gratefully accepted the offering; it was nice to be mothered. She was quite right, he had been so eager to get here that he had overlooked lunch.

The doorbell rang again, Mrs Walmsley went to answer; she showed a young man into the front room, he was about the same height as Geoff wore spectacles with thick lenses and a green corduroy jacket with leather patches on the elbows.

"It's Jim!" Said Chloe's mum.

He walked into the room with an air of familiarity, went over to Chloe and planted a big kiss on her lips in a way that suggested that he was more than just a university colleague. This surprised Geoff, the first time he had heard Chloe make any reference to Jim was on the way to Cromwell's Cave three days earlier and Chloe's actions, on her visit the previous week, hardly suggested that she was romantically involved with anyone.

"It takes all sorts!" thought Geoff.

Mrs Walmsley came back in this time with a plate of sandwiches for Jim "Just cheese for Jim, he doesn't like tomato," she said with a smile, "and tea with two sugars."

Geoff couldn't help thinking that Jim had got both his feet firmly under Chloe's table.

Mrs Walmsley left them to it saying that she had to carry on with the washing.

"You've not met Jim have you Geoff?" said Chloe.

"No!" said Geoff, offering his right hand, "pleased to meet you and thank you for offering to help us."

"Jim's more than pleased to come on board," said Chloe, "he has an interest in the Croxley family."

"I suppose being a historian you'll want to delve into all that medieval scandal?" said Geoff.

"Medieval scandal doesn't come into it," said Jim "I'm interested in more recent goings on," he reached for Chloe's hand "You see Geoff I'm illegitimate, a real, old fashioned bastard and before she died my mother told me that Frank Croxley is my father. She said he raped her"

Geoff was taken aback by this revelation; he was lost for words.

Chloe broke the silence that followed Jim's disclosure, "Now you understand why I thought that involving Brian Clayton, at this stage, was a bad idea. "She beckoned them both to come and sit round the large dining table. Jim opened his briefcase, took out a file and placed it on the table. Chloe took half a dozen or so sheets of foolscap from her bag. "Do you want to start Jim?" she said.

"Will do!" said Jim. "Most of these are copies taken from the Microfiche in the record offices. I've also made some hand-written notes because taking copies from the microfiche is expensive, they charge five pence a sheet."

"Jim let me know what it cost you, I'll pay, no problem." said Geoff.

"That's appreciated," said Jim, "The whole lot cost one pound and five pence."

Geoff gave him two pounds knowing that as a student Jim would have to make every penny count, "Keep the change in case you need to get any more." he said.

"Cheers!" said Jim "I think you'll find that it's money well spent."

"Show me!" said Geoff.

"OK!" said Jim, "But before we get on to the characters involved I think that you will find this interesting," he put two pieces of paper down on the table, they were copies of cuttings, from the Lancashire Evening Telegraph, some years previously. The headline read: -

ROAD PROTESTORS DRUG ORGY
IN CROXLEY'S WOOD

Geoff remembered relating the story to Ali. Several years previously a group of hippies had camped in Croxley's wood in protest against the proposed widening of the main road. Turning it into a dual carriageway would destroy a considerable amount of broad-leaved woodland on the north side of the highway.

Although it was a peaceful protest and the hippies were not doing any harm, Frank Croxley, for reasons best known to himself, called on the local police force to evict the protesters from the woods. The police went in, with dogs and batons at the ready, they were expecting resistance. What they found was a bunch of twelve hippies dancing around, semi-naked, apparently under the influence of some hallucinogenic drug. They were all promptly arrested and marched off to Blackburn police station. They were released the next day when it became evident that the hippies were not in possession of any illegal substances. This was of great embarrassment to Lancashire Constabulary but the local press found it very amusing indeed.

"Do you remember the incident Geoff?" asked Jim.

"Vaguely." said Geoff "I know the police never got to the bottom of it."

"Well somebody did!" exclaimed Jim, "but sometimes people take it upon themselves to keep things in the dark."

"I'm not with you," said Geoff, "what do you mean?"

Chloe butted in, "If someone discovered that a naturally occurring substance was a hallucinogen and was abundant in a local woodland, do you really think that he or she would make that information available to the public?"

"You mean the roses?" said Geoff.

"Not exactly," said Jim "It's not the roses, it's the trees."

Geoff was confused.

Chloe unfolded an Ordnance Survey map that showed The Ribble Valley, and placed it on the table, "Find Croxley's Wood for me." she said to Geoff.

It was quite simple really; Geoff scanned the map and ran his finger along the main road that ran more or less parallel with the thick blue line that represented the River Ribble. His finger stopped on a relatively large green-coloured area. "That's Croxley's wood!" he said, tapping the map.

"What's it called on the map?" asked Jim.

Geoff looked at the italicised wording in the centre of the green area *"The Lirium,"* he said.

"Does that sound like anything else to you?" asked Chloe.

"Nothing springs to mind." said Geoff.

"How about 'delirium'?" said Jim, "It's an adulteration of the word delirium."

It suddenly occurred to Geoff that Chloe and Jim knew a lot more about this Croxley business than they had led him to believe. Now rather than them helping to solve his problem, as was the original intention, he was beginning to feel like a 'missing piece' from one of their jigsaws.

"This has gone far enough," he said "If we're all in this together then we've got to come clean and put all the cards on the table."

Chloe blushed slightly and looked at Jim.

"OK!" aid Jim, he handed the copy of the second newspaper cutting to Geoff, "Do you recognise anyone on that photo?"

Chapter 16

Dodgy dealings.

Geoff looked at the sheet of paper; a photograph of a bunch of hippies smiling from ear to ear took up most of it. The headline read: -

**WOODLAND REVELLERS - DRUGS CHARGES
DROPPED**

The caption underneath the photo read: -

**The eleven accused leave Blackburn Magistrates Court,
jubilant in the knowledge that the charge of 'Being in
possession of illegal substances' has been quashed**

Geoff had to look hard at the photo for a minute or so before it hit him, the two people holding hands, at the end of the line, it was Chloe and Jim. "It's you two!" he said with a grin. "You look like a couple of refugees from Woodstock."

"Those were the days," said Chloe, "peace, love, long hot summers and not a care in the world. We were at Preston Sixth-form College together, Jim and I were an item back then."

"Were!" said Geoff, "It looks to me like you still are."

"No!" said Jim, "although we have remained close friends, we are both 'free spirits' and value our independence too much to get tied down." he went on; "Notice anything else untoward about that second newspaper cutting?"

Geoff looked at it again, "Not really, I certainly don't recognise anyone else."

Chloe pushed the first cutting back across the table towards him. "Look at the numbers." she said.

Geoff cast his eye over the two newspaper cuttings again.

"I think I get your drift," said Geoff, "the first story gives the number as twelve, arrested, the second article reports eleven released. What happened to the twelfth person then?"

"It was a girl!" Said Jim. "They took her along to the station, with the rest of us. When we arrived a lawyer, complete with pinstripe suit and briefcase, pointed her out. She followed him into an interview room and that was the last the rest of us saw of her, she had connections in high places who used their influence to get her off the hook."

"Who was she?" said Geoff.

"Her name was Christina." Said Jim

"You probably know her as Tina, Tina Clayton or Croxley as she was then." Said Chloe.

"Brian's wife!" exclaimed Geoff.

"And my estranged half sister." said Jim.

"It was Tina's idea to set up the protest in the first place." Chloe explained, "She didn't really give a monkeys about the dual carriageway she just wanted to make sure that her precious 'magic' roses weren't destroyed by progress."

"She knew about the effect of the roses then?" asked Geoff.

"Yes!" said Chloe; "when Brian told you that it was 'a secret old Croxley family concoction' he was telling you the truth, they've been using it for years, even before the family name changed from Croxleigh."

"The thing is," interrupted Jim, "it's not actually the roses that cause the effect."

"Go on!" said Geoff.

"It comes from a fungus that grows on the leaves of the trees high above; it appears as dark round circular blotches, about a quarter of an inch in diameter, on the leaves. The spores contain a 'psilicybin' type substance like that which is found in so-called 'magic mushrooms,' it's a hallucinogenic toxin that is known to stimulate psychic perception. The fungus ripens at the same time as the roses below bloom and because the spores are heavier than air, many of them fall and settle on the rose bushes below. This results in the rose petals being coated in a substance which can cause severe psychotropic poisoning in large doses or a feeling of well-being or mild hallucination if ingested in lesser quantities."

"Why has no-one else cottoned on to this?" asked Geoff, "surely Croxley's Wood isn't the only woods with wild roses growing beneath Oak trees?"

"They're not just ordinary Oak trees," said Chloe "they're quite unique really they; are a hybrid or cross between English Oak and another Oak that grows in Mediterranean areas. It's not uncommon for the two to hybridise but usually the resulting tree is sterile; however the ones in Croxley's Wood are fertile, they flower and seed freely, it's some interaction between the flower and the leaf that encourages the fungus.

"So who knows about this? The Police?" asked Geoff.

"We don't think so," said Chloe, "we know that ever since the incident, when we all got arrested, Stan Croxley has taken an interest in the woods."

"Could this be part of the reason why he's had the gateway made more secure?"

"Possibly, he may have found out that you've been in there, he doesn't like people going into Croxley's Wood, that's why he got a court order slapped on the eleven protesters to prevent us going in again." said Chloe.

"Seems a bit over the top." said Geoff.

"Not if you're protecting your source of income," said Jim.

"I'm not with you," said Geoff.

Jim enlightened him; "Stan's gone into the drugs business." He said.

"The boxes!" exclaimed Geoff suddenly. "Chloe I forgot to mention the collecting boxes, there were lots of them in the wood, on the ground, in amongst the bracken."

Jim's eyes lit up, "Describe one!" he said, with an air of excitement in his voice.

"Give me a sheet of paper and I'll draw on for you." said Geoff.

Chloe produced a blank sheet of A4 paper and a pencil, she gave it to Geoff "An artist too!" She said, with a smile, "You do hide your many lights under a bushel."

Geoff sketched the tray, "That's the best I can do, from memory," he said, "but give or take half an inch, or so, on the size, that's a reasonable representation."

Jim examined the sketch "No doubt about it," he said, "these are devices designed to catch the spores as they float down towards the ground. The mesh will stop leaves or other large pieces of debris entering the catchment container and the funnel shape will ensure that, when it rains, the spores are washed down through the debris and trapped on the filter paper below, like it does on the rose petals."

"How does Croxley turn it into a usable product?" asked Geoff, "surely he will need some sort of laboratory?"

"Not at all!" said Jim "there will be a pale brown crud that forms on top of the filter paper, this will be quite a concentrated form of the substance. Once allowed to dry out it could be carefully scraped off and stored in powder form or, as I suspect, left on the filter paper which is cut up into half-inch squares wrapped in cellophane and sold as it is." He went on, "when you think that a half-inch square would probably be the equivalent of fifty or sixty times the dose that you got from the rose petals you can appreciate it's quite a potent drug."

"So how much is he making out of this little enterprise?" asked Geoff.

"Stan will sell it straight to the dealers who then fix a street value of between five and ten pounds a square, depending on where you buy it." Said Jim.

"He's not going to make a fortune then?" said Geoff.

"Think about it," said Chloe, "each collection box contains a filter paper two foot square, that's two thousand three hundred an four half-inch squares in each box."

"I assume that Stan will ask the dealers to pay him two pounds per square so that works out at over four and a half grand per tray; multiply that by the number of trays and it certainly adds up.

"So we've established that there are some dodgy dealings going on in Croxley's Wood," said Geoff, " But what's the connection with Rose and Bryan of Clayton?"

Chloe answered him, "We just thought that you needed to know what you were getting into, messing with the Croxley's, they have a history of being real nasty bastards who don't let anything get in their way. You should bear that in mind the next time you climb over their gates."

"You don't believe me do you?" said Geoff "You think I'm making it all up, about Rose and the dream and the sixth verse of the song, don't you?"

"I've got to admit," said Jim, "I found it a little hard to swallow when Chloe asked me to help but I went along with it because she was convinced that there was some substance to your story. Who am I to argue? I've known Chloe for years, she's a very rational person and not easily taken in."

"So you're just damn well humouring me then?" Snapped Geoff.

Jim smiled at Chloe.

"Tell him!" she said.

"Well I may have had you down for a crackpot, at first," said Jim, "But now I've done some digging I'm inclined to give you the benefit of the doubt."

"You mean you've found something?" said Geoff excitedly.

"Well we can certainly confirm that your characters existed," said Chloe, "I'll put the kettle on and we'll tell you about it over a cuppa."

Chapter 17

Family affairs.

Jim opened his file, it contained a number of sheets copied from the microfiche, some crystal-clear, others so faded that they were almost illegible. Several of them had passages and paragraphs highlighted by being under-lined with a red pencil. None of the sheets contained any photos or pictures, just various styles of text.

"It's a bit like doing a jigsaw," said Jim "You find small pieces of information and try to make them fit together to form the bigger picture."

"I was never much good at jigsaws," said Geoff , "even when I was a kid, I never had the patience."

"Let me give you the picture then," said Jim, "It's about ninety per-cent complete but at least I've got all the straight pieces that go around the edge and most of the bits in the middle, so to speak."

"It's early in the eighteenth century I can't be exact but my research suggests that the following events took place between 1714 and 1720. I base this on the fact that Sir Frederick Croxleigh disappeared without trace in 1720, one line of thought thinks that he may have been murdered in revenge for some indiscretion, possibly connected with our story. There is also a record of one 'Bryan O' Clayton' playing at Samlesbury Hall in 1714."

"We can assume that Bryan O' Clayton and Bryan of Clayton are one and the same then?" asked Geoff.

"That's a pretty safe bet," said Jim, "and considering you first came across the name in a dream I think it's amazing, if not just a little scary."

"Carry on!" said Geoff.

"I couldn't find any more references to Bryan O' Clayton but interestingly enough the Croxleigh file contains several references to 'The Minstrel'."

"Did you find any references to Rose?" asked Geoff.

"There are references to Rosemary and Rosemarie, I'm quite certain they are one and the same person." said Jim.

Chloe butted in: "The records at Whalley Abbey indicate that the convent at Monkswood Lane was destroyed, by a bunch of thugs, who were hired by Croxleigh, in 1719. The nuns had no choice but to up-sticks and move on."

"Well that's another couple of pieces fitted into the puzzle." Said Jim.

He went on: "Rosemary, it appears, was the illegitimate daughter of one Lord Wignall, a landowner from Staffordshire who often passed this way on business. Apparently he always made a point of stopping at Croxleigh Hall because he had the hots for one of the servants who eventually bore his child - Rosemary. Lord Wignall was the exception to the rule, as far as eighteenth century noblemen went, inasmuch as he had a conscience and a sense of duty. It may have been due to the fact that Lady Wignall was barren and could not produce children, which made Lord Wignall take an interest in Rose's upbringing. He made an arrangement with the Croxleigh's and Rose was brought up as their daughter. Lord Wignall still made regular visits to Rose's mother and always took an active interest in the girl's upbringing. Rose's mother's status changed from servant to nanny so that she could have active role in the upbringing of her own child."

"So to the world outside Rose was a Croxleigh?" said Geoff.

"She certainly was!" said Jim.

"Any mention of a Gerald Croxleigh?" asked Geoff.

"I was coming to that next," said Jim, "Sir Frederick Croxleigh had two sons: Charles and Gerald."

Geoff was beginning to feel a little uncomfortable with this, after all Jim was confirming that the facts, which, up until now, had been nothing more than figments of his imagination, actually had some substance.

Jim went on, "One of the Croxleigh boys allegedly raped Rose and put her in the family way. The records don't say which one but I think from the account of your conversation with Rose and the fact that he disappeared at about the same time as his father, we can safely assume that it was Gerald." Jim continued, "Charles went on to run things at Croxleigh Hall, he didn't bother with a title and changed the name to Croxley which suggests that there was something to cover up."

Chloe was getting excited about the story now, "Any mention of a romantic connection between Rose and Bryan of Clayton?" she asked, with a glint of anticipation in her eye.

"No!" said Jim, " I can't find anything definite but he does get a mention."

"In what respect?" asked Geoff.

"The minstrel's song!" Said Jim; "Remember these were the days before mass media' there weren't even newspapers so one of the best ways of hearing news was to listen to the stories and songs that were performed by the local street musicians and performers. These people did the circuits, travelling around the district, from castle to mansion to stately hall, providing entertainment for the rich people at banquets and other such functions. On their journeys, between these functions, which could often take two or three days, if they were on foot, they would often stop along the way and sing for their suppers at village inns and other hostelries. People then were no different than today, they loved to listen to a bit of juicy gossip especially if it was about the lord of the manor. The minstrels would take the opportunity to sing about what they had seen whilst being in the big houses. A song that made light of the local gentry's behaviour would always be well accepted by the rabble. Event the subjects who were ribbed in the songs often took it as a compliment to be thought newsworthy enough to appear in a 'street musical'."

"However the minstrel, who I think we can say beyond doubt was your Bryan of Clayton, overstepped the mark for some reason and sang something that really upset the Croxleigh's."

"Like what?" said Geoff.

"I'm theorising now," said Jim, "So bear with me."

"Suppose that after confirming that Rose was pregnant by his son, who, to the world outside, was Rose's brother, Croxleigh arranged for Rose to be conveniently placed out of the way and had her put in the care of the nuns at the local convent?"

"How have you come to that conclusion?" asked Geoff.

Chloe interrupted, "It was common practice to put young single pregnant women into the care of the church, especially if the father was from the upper classes because in those cases it was always considered that the girl was a sinner. It was only the working class lads that were imprisoned, or worse, for rape."

"I think the minstrel got wind of this." Said Jim, he went on. "Listening to Brian Clayton's version of 'The Rose Of The Ribble Valley,' which by now I think we all agree was certainly written by Bryan of Clayton, the words suggest that the minstrel was singing to Rose, his sweetheart. If on his next visit to Croxleigh Hall he found out what had been going on his absence, then, to say the least, he would have been more than a little pissed off, especially if his beloved Rose was nowhere to be found."

"So by singing about the situation, old Bryan has really opened a can of worms." said Chloe.

"In what way?" Asked Geoff.

"Well!" said Jim, "First of all Croxleigh wouldn't have been pleased about the fact that his youngest sons raping of his 'sister' was becoming common knowledge. And secondly Lord Wignall would have been most upset, not only by the fact that his only child had been abused by a member of the family with whom he had entrusted her welfare, but because the whole thing was now 'out in the open' his wife, Lady Wignall, may find out the truth."

"This all sounds plausible but we're still speculating aren't we?" said Geoff.

"Yes we are." said Jim "But what if I added that the Wignalls divorced in 1723 on the grounds of Lord Wignall's infidelity?"

"That's about the right sort of time-scale for the legalities," said Chloe, "Even though it was legal, getting divorced in the eighteenth century wasn't as simple as it is today, it could take several years."

"Those are the facts, as far as we have them," said Jim, "Would you like a breakdown of what I think happened?"

"You've certainly done alright so far," said Geoff "Carry on!"

"OK," said Jim, "here it is."

He unfolded a sheet of A3 paper and placed it on the table. The heading said "Rose of the Ribble Valley, circa 1714-1720 AD." Underneath there was a bulleted list of Jim's conclusions/theories.

- Bryan of Clayton meets Rosemary during his travels up and down the Ribble Valley. They become lovers and Bryan composes the song "Rose of the Ribble Valley" to publicly demonstrate his feelings for her. He proposes marriage, she accepts, however Croxleigh will not go along with this relationship for two reasons. Firstly the outside world thinks that Rosemary is a Croxleigh and she couldn't be seen to marry a 'common entertainer'. Secondly Lord Wignall, who puts a lot of business Croxleigh's way, would be upset if his 'only child' married a 'low life'.

- Pressure is put upon Bryan to stop him seeing Rose. Croxleigh probably asks his acquaintances and other landowners in the valley to stop booking the singer so as to block his earning capacity, making it very difficult for Bryan to carry out any plans to wed Rose.

- Rose finds out that Croxleigh is trying to force Bryan's hand and during the ensuing family arguments, the fact that Rose is not actually a Croxleigh is revealed to Gerald and Charles. This suddenly puts their relationship into a whole new ball game and Gerald makes romantic advances towards Rose. She tells him where to get off; he takes her by force.

- Croxleigh is furious; now that Rose's secret is out in the open she has no loyalty to him or his family and she is determined that Gerald should get his come-uppance for raping her. Croxleigh arranges for her to taken to Monkswood Convent and placed in care of the nuns where she will be kept quiet until he can sort things out.
- Bryan returns to Croxleigh Hall in an attempt to see Rose. Obviously she is not there and the Croxleighs refuse to have anything whatsoever to do with him, let alone tell him of Rose's fate. However tongues wag and one of the servants (maybe Rose's natural mother) tells him what has happened. Bryan can't get anywhere near the Croxleighs so he decides to start a smear campaign; he composes an extra verse to his song and sings it wherever he goes. The people put two and two together and gossip spreads like wildfire.
- Croxleigh kills, or pays someone to kill Bryan of Clayton In an attempt to try and suppress the story; they hide the corpse so as to make it appear that Bryan has left the area in search of work. Rose starts making noises at the monastery (she must have got wind of Bryans disappearance) and manages to get word to Lord Wignall.
- Before Wignall turns up, Croxleigh arranges for Roses Death (probably by poisoning so that it appears to be a complication with the pregnancy). The nuns realise that something is amiss and start to voice their suspicions and concerns. Croxleigh has them run off his land and destroys the convent.
- Wignall gets his revenge and employs someone to 'do away' with Croxleigh and his youngest son Gerald.

"Looks feasible to me," said Geoff, "You've certainly done your homework Jim, thanks very much."

"I just wish that you could recall the words to the extra verse," said Jim "It may have given us something else to work on."

"We still don't know what Rose wants though, do we?" said Chloe.

"I know," said Geoff, "It's obvious: Rose doesn't know what happened to Bryan and he certainly didn't know what happened to her and neither of them can rest in peace until they know the fate and resting place of the other."

"You seem reasonably confident about that," said Jim, almost jokingly, "You haven't been talking to Bryan of Clayton in your sleep too, have you?"

"No I haven't!" said Geoff." I know because of what was scratched on the log in Croxley's Wood. It said 'Please help find us, we are lost!' and as far as I'm concerned that is a plea for help from beyond the grave, and furthermore I'm positive that she is buried underneath the log in Croxley's Wood."

"What makes you so sure?" asked Chloe.

"In the dream she was shocked to see me sitting on the log and after I gave her a lift home, from Cromwell's Cave, she wanted to return there and then there was the rose and the inscription."

"Well it's not much," said Jim, " but it's all we've got; I'll buy it! When do you want to go and dig?"

Chapter 18

If you go down in the woods today.

It was very early on Sunday morning; Chloe parked the car far enough down Monkswood Lane so as not to be seen from the main road. She opened the boot and Geoff took out the canvas bag that contained the spades, a fork and the rest of Chloe's archaeological dig paraphernalia. Jim unhooked the bungees from the roof rack and motioned to Chloe to grab the other end of the short tapering ladder that Geoff had borrowed from his window cleaner. The air was full of the sound of the dawn chorus and there wasn't another soul or car in sight as they made their way across the main road to where the newly fortified gates seemed to threaten anyone who dared to enter within.

Jim took the ladder from Geoff and placed it against the wall next to the gates, he climbed up and straddled the stonework. He beckoned to Geoff to pass up the bag, which he hoisted over the wall and dropped down into the undergrowth on the other side. The loud 'clank' made by the spades frightened the two hundred or so rooks that were roosting in the trees above, they took off in unison 'cawing' loudly. Geoff looked up at Jim.

"Don't worry," said Jim, "they do that every morning as soon as the first car goes past in daylight." Then, as if on cue, an old Vauxhall drove by.

Chloe was next up the ladder, when she got onto the top of the wall Jim pulled up the ladder and lowered it down the other side. He helped Chloe back onto the ladder and she climbed down into the woods. He lifted up the ladder again and put it back against the outside of the wall to allow Geoff to climb up.

Soon all three of them were stood inside Croxley's Wood.

They made their way along the bracken-covered track up to the clearing; the rose bushes were all in bud. Jim was the first to discover one of Stan Croxley's collecting boxes, it was a carbon copy of Geoff's experience a few days earlier, Jim let out a loud "BASTARD" when the when the sharp edge of the box hit his shin. Almost immediately the ground, about ten feet in front of them, erupted as a deer and her fawn, terrified by Jim's outburst, stood up and made a bolt for it. Three hearts simultaneously missed a beat, after which they looked at each other and started laughing with relief.

They came upon half a dozen more collecting boxes before they arrived at the log, and there, resting on top of it, just like during Geoff's previous visit, was a single pink rose. It was in exactly the same place, adjacent to the carved inscription. Geoff couldn't believe his eyes, the inscription was there but now it read "Thank you'" with no trace of any previous inscription showing on the smooth bark. He took the rose and put it into his pocket.

The oak log was about three and a half feet in diameter and eight feet long and although it was roughly circular, in cross section, the knobbly protrusions where the branches had been broken off would make it difficult to roll away, even with three of them pushing it.

"It's just about the right size to cover a grave," said Chloe, "How are we going to move it?"

"We'll need to lever it up and push at the same time," said Geoff.

"How about using these?" said Jim.

He took the two spades and the fork out of the large bag and gave the fork to Chloe and one of the spades to Geoff; he kept hold of one of the spades himself.

"Be careful," he said, "We don't want any more like this!" He rolled up his trouser-leg to reveal a large bloody graze, on his shin, where the skin had been knocked off during his collision with the collecting box.

"Poor thing!" said Chloe, "They say fools rush in where angels fear to tread."

"Not bloody funny!" said Jim. But of course it was and all three of them roared with laughter.

They tried to move the log, Chloe and Jim at each end with Geoff in the middle. They pushed the spades and fork, as far as they could, under the log, and tried to manoeuvre it forward by pushing whilst levering at the same time. It was futile; the log would only move an inch or so then the levers would sink into the rotten wood, on the bottom of the log causing it to crumble and allowing the log to roll back to its starting point.

"We need a longer lever," said Geoff, "Something strong and rigid that we can get right beneath the log."

"The ladder!" said Jim, "Chloe and I will go back for the ladder, you dig out a space underneath the log so that we can get it in."

Geoff scraped away at a point roughly in the middle of the log, where the rotting wood met the ground. The consistency of the earth was more like a soft peat than hard clay, which made the digging very easy indeed. He was about halfway through when the spade made a grating sound indicating that he had hit something hard, probably a stone. He took out a couple of spade-loads and carefully sieved through them in an attempt to find whatever it was that had made the noise. His fingers searched the pile of earth and locked on to a solid object, he shook off all the debris and tapped it gently on the log in front of him. It appeared to be a piece of rusty tube, about ten inches long tapering in diameter from about three-quarters to a quarter of an inch. There were three holes drilled in it, one on top and two underneath, running length-wise.

He heard the rustling sound of feet walking through bracken and stood up and turned around, expecting to see Chloe and Jim. They were there all right but what he wasn't expecting was the two burly uniformed security guards who were accompanying them.

"Put the spade down sonny," said the guard who had a tight grip on Jim's arm.

Geoff dropped the spade to the ground whilst discreetly slipping the metal tube into his pocket.

The other guard, who held Chloe tightly by the collar of her anorak said, sarcastically, "Digging for truffles are we?"

Geoff treated the remark with the contempt it deserved and decided that the best course of action was to say and do nothing.

The first guard let go of Jim "Gather your stuff together, you three are coming with us."

Jim held the neck of the large canvass bag open while Geoff put the tools back inside.

The first guard unclipped a radio that was attached to his belt. Geoff looked at him; he was six feet tall and built like a tank, not the sort of chap to tangle with. On the shoulder of his uniform was a cloth badge with "Ribble Valley Security" and the familiar red rose symbol embroidered on it. The guard lifted the radio up to his face and pressed the 'speak' button.

"Alpha three here! Can you patch me through to the governor?" There was a loud static crackle from the radio over the top of the reply, which sounded like "OK Jack you're through."

"Morning Mr C, We've got three of those badger baiters down here in the clearing, one of the lads who works at the warehouse had seen them climbing the wall on his way to work"

Again the radio made a loud crackling noise, this time Geoff couldn't make out the reply. "Will do! Out!" said the guard.

"Right! Follow me," said the first guard "Let's make this easy, no funny business, you can't get out of the woods without us and if you try and run for it you could hurt yourself, know what I mean?" He picked up a branch and violently snapped it over his knee.

They all got the message and followed the guard down the bracken-covered track back to the wall, his colleague brought up the rear.

When they got to the wall the first guard climbed over, there were now two ladders; the one belonging to Geoff's window-cleaner on the wood side and a shiny new aluminium one on the road side. Geoff went next followed by Chloe, then Jim and finally the second guard.

"We're off your property now!" said Geoff "I take it that means we're free to go?"

"Not quite!" said the first guard. A Mercedes, with dark tinted windows, pulled up behind the Croxley Security van that was parked with two wheels on the verge.

Chapter 19

Call my bluff.

Stanislaw Croxley climbed out of the Mercedes and approached the group on the verge, he didn't venture too close in case he got dirt on his shoes or the bottom of his trouser legs. He wore a beige coloured 'Crombie' style mohair coat, sunglasses and a pair of brown leather gloves; attire more akin to a West-end villain than a Lancashire country gentleman.

"Well, well, look who we've got here then," he said, looking at the trio "Sonny and fucking Cher and Clayton's lapdog."

The second guard emptied the tools, out of the canvass bag, onto the ground. "They were digging boss, figured they must be after badgers!"

"So that's why you and your friends were so keen to protect the woodland then?" said Stan sarcastically, "You like exterminating the wildlife!" he gave an evil grin.

Geoff interrupted "Stan it's not like that…"

"Fucking shut it!" barked Stan, "I've got the chair here, and you're the bad guys! Remember? Can't you read the signs: 'Private Woodland. Keep Out'."

"There's a court injunction stopping you two trespassing on Croxley property." He said, pointing at Chloe and Jim. "He's got an excuse," this time pointing at Geoff. "He's a mate of Clayton's so he must be a thick twat!"

Geoff wasn't prone to violence but Stan had gone too far. He stepped forward and tried to grab Stan by the lapels but before he knew what had hit him the first guard had grabbed him and held him in a 'hammer lock' with his hand firmly up his back.

"We're no more interested in digging for badgers than you are in protecting them," said Jim.

"So what the fuck are you doing in my woods then?" said Croxleigh.

It was Chloe's turn to say her piece: "Actually Mr Croxley we were doing some historical research, I'm with the archaeological department up at Lancaster University and, as you probably know, your father allowed us to dig on the old Monkswood site."

"What's that got to do with the woods?" asked Stan.

Jim got the drift of what Chloe was trying to do and jumped in. "We were comparing soil samples and such, to try and establish whether or not the oak beams, used in the construction at Monkswood, were made from local wood. As you know the woods used to stretch right down to the river but there's not much of it left north of the road." He went on, "We needed a sample of some old dead wood, we knew about the clearing so it seemed the obvious solution. The university don't know about the previous incident, you know, the protest, so we thought it would save any embarrassment if we sneaked in quietly, rather than re-opening an old can of worms."

"What's he doing here then?" asked Croxley, pointing to Geoff, who was still being held by the guard.

"We just borrowed his ladder and he decided to come along for the ride." Said Chloe.

"He's going to get a ride all right!" said Croxley, "In the back of the Old Bills van, call 'em Jack!" he said to the guard with the radio. He looked back at the trio "Badger baiting carries a heavy penalty you know!"

"Hang on Stan!" said Geoff. "All right we should have asked you if we could go into the woods, but we didn't, and now you've caught us red handed and we find ourselves in a very embarrassing situation."

"What the fuck are you going on about?" said Stan.

"The collecting boxes!" said Geoff.

"Forget the call for a minute Jack." said Croxley to the guard who was just about to contact the police. "Go on," he said to Geoff.

"If we go to the police station, we'd have to tell them about the collecting boxes. It could be very embarrassing for you if the police found out that someone was collecting large amounts of psilicybin which, if used for 'recreational' purposes, would contravene the drug laws."

Stan's face began to colour-up a little; he wasn't the most intelligent man in the world and Geoff's little speech had stopped him in his tracks.

"I don't know fuck all about them boxes," said Stan with an expression on his face that was saying "Guilty your honour."

Geoff humoured him, "I'm sure that you don't Stan, it's just that if we were to have to make a statement down at the cop shop then we'd have to mention the cut on Jim's shin and what caused it, show him Jim."

Jim rolled up his trouser leg and displayed the dried up bloody graze "The thing is Stan, that after I'd stood on the one that did this, we had look around and there's dozens of the things. I'm sure that if the police knew then they'd want to go trampling all over your woods."

Stan changed his tune; "Ok he said we'll let it go this time, call this a warning but if I catch you in there again I might not be as reasonable next time. Take your stuff and fuck off."

Geoff picked up the bag while Jim retrieved the wooden ladder. They made their way along the verge toward Monkswood Lane where Chloe's car was parked. They had to allow the Mercedes and the Croxley Security van to pass before they could cross the carriageway.

"You played a blinder there mate," said Jim to Geoff, "I thought we'd had it for sure."

The only problem now is that we won't find out whether or not Rose is buried under the log," said Chloe as they climbed into the car.

"She's not!" said Geoff, "Bryan of Clayton is."

"How do you know that?" said Jim.

Geoff took the small rusting tube out of his pocket and held it up.

"What's that?" asked Chloe.

"It's a galoubet." Said Geoff. "An early version of a tin whistle that could be played with one hand, leaving the other hand free to drum, standard kit for an eighteenth century street musician."

"Well!" exclaimed Chloe, "If Bryan's under the log, where's Rose?"

Chapter 20

Abigail.

It was the day of Lute's benefit concert and a capacity crowd was expected due to the coverage that it had received in the local Media. Radio Lancashire had done a telephone interview with Geoff and the band and the Post and the Telegraph had both given the event good publicity.

Geoff had arranged for the band to get down early so that they could sound-check using the system that Charlie Bagwell was providing for them. He had asked Pushing Forté and Woody to be there early too, so that they could all go through the last minute things like times and running orders.

Chloe had invited Jim along to the concert and had offered to pick him up; that meant that Geoff had to find his own way there.

It was about half past four when Geoff pulled onto the small car park outside the Grey Mare; Wayne's car was already there, parked next to a Transit van that had its back doors open. Wayne was stood at the back of the van with his arms around each side of a large speaker cabinet that someone else, stood inside the back of the van, was manoeuvring slowly outwards. Geoff jumped out of the car and went to assist Wayne.

"Take it easy mate," said Geoff, "I can't be doing with my bass player having two broken arms."

"I'm quite capable of doing this myself!" It was a female voice from the back of the van. A girl's head appeared over the top of the speaker cabinet and looked down onto the two musicians. "Surely it doesn't take two men to do a woman's job?" she said with a beaming smile.

"That's our 'Soundman'!" said Wayne with a grin.

Geoff laughed as he looked at the somehow familiar face that was smiling at him from the back of the van. He grabbed the handle on one side of the speaker and Wayne took hold of the other. They lifted it out of the van and placed it on the ground. Geoff offered his hand to the girl to help her out of the van. She declined the offer.

"I'm a big girl now!" she said sarcastically

"You're not kidding." thought Geoff to himself as he admired the way she filled the T-shirt that had: -

"MARSHALL AMPLIFICATION" emblazoned across the front of it. He then realised where he had seen her before.

"It's Velvet isn't it? He asked.

"Yes it is!" she said, "but that's my 'stage name' you can call me Abigail, Abigail Bagwell."

"Charlie's Daughter?" said Geoff.

"His niece actually," said Abigail.

"No bloody wonder Charlie got upset when I slagged her off at the Malt Shovel." thought Geoff.

"I'm Geoff!" he said, offering his hand again.

This time she accepted "And what do you do Geoff?"

"I'm a Folk-singer!" he said.

"Hmm that's different, I've never slept with a Folk-singer." said Abigail.

"Chance would be a fine thing!" said Geoff, not knowing whether the girl was teasing him or being genuinely suggestive. One thing for sure was that he would have some fun finding out.

"Are you going to stand there all day or are we going to carry this thing in?" asked Wayne, as he beckoned to Geoff to grab the other side of the cabinet. They lifted it up and carried it carefully up the stone steps and through the door of the concert room.

The stage was full of sound equipment: two large heavy power amps that were mounted in a black metallic rack; two bass speakers, which where much larger than the one that they had just brought in; a mixing desk; a large crate containing what looked like miles of cables and of course the other speaker that matched the one that they had just carried.

"Looks like you've been busy." Geoff said to Wayne.

"Not me mate!" said Wayne, "I only arrived a couple of minutes before you did.

Slightly embarrassed, they both turned to look at Abigail.

"I really don't know how I would have managed if you two big strong men hadn't turned up to help me with that last speaker." she said.

"Sarcasm is a very low form of wit!" said Wayne.

"Men are only good for one thing!" she said, as she extended her arm out towards them and stuck her middle finger up in the air. She smiled and said "Would you like me to show you how it all fits together then?"

"I think you've made your point," said Geoff.

"Good!" she said, "So now you can do another manly thing and go get a lady a drink."

Geoff walked through to the bar it was empty. There was no sign of Brian or Tina but Geoff knew that they must be around somewhere otherwise Abigail wouldn't have been able to get in.

There was a large brass bell hanging on the rail above the bar, it was probably there so that the barman could ring 'Last Orders' and 'Time Gentlemen Please'. Geoff pulled three times on the red and gold chord that was attached to the striker; the bell rang out.

The bamboo curtain, at the end of the bar, rattled as it parted in the middle. The first thing that came through was a hand carrying a steaming coffee mug, it was closely followed by the rest of Brian, who looked like he had a bit of a sweat on.

"Geoff! How goes it?" he said, wiping his forehead with his sleeve, "I was just grabbing a couple of minutes, I'm absolutely knackered after helping that lass cart her stuff in."

Geoff laughed out loud "That's one-nil to her then," he said. "She had Wayne and me believing that she'd carried it in all by herself."

Tina came through the curtain, she was laughing aloud, "Nice to see that a young lass wearing a tight T-shirt can still manage to manipulate three grown men" she said.

"Well we couldn't watch her struggle," said Brian.

"Really!" said Tina smiling," and I thought that it was just some macho desire to impress."

Tina unrolled the fluorescent orange poster that she was carrying, it was three feet high and eighteen inches wide, written on it in thick black felt tip was: -

BENEFIT CONCERT SPECIAL
HOME-MADE
LANCASHIRE HOT POT
75P
PLEASE ORDER
AT THE BAR.

"We thought that a bit of food wouldn't go amiss," said Tina.

"It's a great idea!" Said Geoff "And it will add to the total."

"Hang on a minute," said Brian, "the hot-pot money goes into the till, we do have a business to run you know!"

Geoff was a bit taken aback by this; after all he was providing free entertainment and a guaranteed 'full house' consisting of a 'Folky' type audience who traditionally drank lots of beer. Surely it wasn't too much to expect some sort of gesture from the Landlord and Landlady However now was not the time to get into that sort of debate, there were instruments to be tuned, sounds to check and running orders to sort.

Geoff returned to the concert room with three glasses of Coca-Cola, it was still early in the day and the fact that he was driving meant that he would have to keep an eye on his intake of beer.

The speakers were now in position on either side of the stage, neatly piled on top of each other, like children's building bricks; the large bass bins at the bottom, the small treble horns on top and the mid range cabs in the middle. The mixing desk was on a table to the right of the stage, far enough forward to allow Abigail to listen to what the audience were hearing and make any necessary adjustments to the sound.

Wayne was testing the middle one of the three microphones set up at the front of the stage "ONE TWO -

115

ONE TWO" boomed out through the loudspeakers, intermingled with the annoying sound of 'feedback' which whistled so loudly that it hurt Geoff's ears. Abigail, with all the cool of a professional, was adjusting the volume and tone sliders, on the mixing desk, to try and achieve a balanced sound.

Geoff put the Cola down on the table beside the mixing desk and looked at Abigail. "This is a folk concert! He shouted, tapping his ear. "Not bleeding Woodstock."

Abigail hit the stand-by button and stood up as the humming stopped. "If you think that you can do any better be my guest," she said offering him the chair; she picked up the glass of Coke and thrust it into his face "And the first rule is, no drinks near the equipment!"

Wayne's laughter didn't need any amplification to fill the room, "Geoff go and tune your guitar up outside and leave us alone 'til we're ready for you."

"That sounds like a bloody good idea," said Abigail.

Geoff held his hand up "OK, you win," he said to Abigail; then to Wayne "Careful she bites!"

"Only when I get really mad," said Abigail. "Look Geoff I know what I'm doing pull up a chair and I'll explain."

Wayne was still smiling.

Geoff sat down beside Abigail at the mixing desk, he really had no idea whatsoever about amplification and was usually quite happy to let Wayne sort it out. Abigail explained that, first of all, acoustically, every room was different and what seemed loud in a relatively empty room would not seem loud at all when the same room was full of people. She went on to explain that she needed to set the sound as loud as possible without feedback so that during the evening she would have room to manoeuvre. If she needed to turn up the volume for any reason she had to be confident that she wouldn't get any feedback, which was not only unprofessional it also made the listeners, in the audience, uncomfortable.

Geoff pretended to understand what she talking about and nodded.

"Am I forgiven for shouting then?" she said looking him straight in the eye.

"I suppose so," he said

"Good! Then maybe we can be friends," she said as her fingers gave the inside of his thigh a seductive squeeze.

Chapter 21

A surprise guest.

By ten minutes to six Abigail was satisfied with the sound; she had sorted out the levels on the three microphones and balanced them with Geoff's guitar and mandolin, and with Wayne's bass.

"What time are the others arriving?" She asked.

"I've told them to be here as soon after six as possible," said Geoff.

"They'd better be here soon if they want a proper sound check," said Abigail.

" Pushing Forté won't be a problem!" said Wayne, "Steve's guitar has a good quality pick-up on it, I've never had a problem plugging him in. Woody's a different kettle of fish though, he doesn't plug in so we'll have to put a microphone on his guitar."

"Can't he borrow Geoff's or Steve's?" said Abigail.

"Not really" said Wayne "he's strictly a blues player and has spent a lot of time and effort into getting his guitar to produce the right sound."

"We'll just have to do our best," said Abigail.

As far as Geoff was concerned they may as well have been speaking a foreign language he went back through to the bar, rang the bell and ordered three beers from Brian. He took the beers back through to the concert room and suggested that the three of them take a break and have their drinks outside.

They sat around a table on the sunny side of the bowling greens.

"How come Velvet's not performing anywhere tonight then?" Geoff asked Abigail.

"Velvet doesn't exist anymore," said Abigail. "She was just someone who was manufactured by Uncle Charles."

"You mean you've packed it in then?" Said Geoff.

"Certainly have," said Abigail, "but then I'm a realist and I know I haven't got a voice and the last straw was when the

Concert Secretary, at the Spinning Wheel Workingmen's Club, in Blackburn, said that he was paying me off, at half time, unless I was prepared to get my kit off and do the second half topless."

Wayne nearly choked on his beer, "Well in that case I would have certainly stayed and listened" he said.

The three of them burst into fits of laughter.

They had no sooner finished their drinks than the rest of the performers arrived almost simultaneously; Chloe arrived with Jim, and Woody had brought Steve and Carol Whalley from Pushing Forté.

Abigail was on the ball, she had them sound checked in no time at all. The next thing was to sort the running order.

Geoff had decided that Elderflower punch would start the proceedings and play for twenty minutes from eight thirty until eight fifty. Woody would do the second spot from eight fifty-five until nine twenty. There would then be a break for the raffle.

Pushing Forté would start the second half at nine forty and do half an hour then Elderflower punch would do their main spot, taking proceedings up to about ten past eleven when they would invite Steve, Carol and Woody to join them on stage to finish off with a 'rip-roarer'.

Dave and Julie Jackson turned up at twenty past seven and came straight to the concert room, Julie had agreed to sell raffle tickets and Dave said that he would help Jim look after the door.

People had started to arrive; they all went into the lounge bar for their first drink, the doors to the concert room wouldn't actually open until 7:45.

Abigail said that she could play background music during the audience's arrival; Geoff thought it was a good idea.

"We'll start with this one especially for you then," she said as she inserted a CD. It was Carol Kings' *Will you still love me tomorrow,* and the words *'Tonight You're Mine Completely'* came through the speakers.

Geoff couldn't help thinking that maybe this was turning out to be a great night in more ways than one.

The doors opened and the audience started to come through. Dave and Jim were working frantically taking the entry fees from people as they arrived. Several raffle prizes were donated, these were left at the door with Dave and Jim, these included; a large cuddly teddy bear, a bottle of Bells whisky, two boxes of chocolates and half a dozen bottles of wine.

Looking at the faces of the people arriving, Geoff recognised the majority of them as people who attended Elderflower Punch concerts and other 'folky' events in the area. However he was surprised by one of the attendees.

"What does that twat want?" he said to Wayne and pointed at Stan Croxley taking a fiver out of his wallet and giving it to Jim, on the door. He was partnered by a woman of about forty whom, from the way she was dressed, looked like she was bound for a 'Society Ball' and not a Folk Evening.

"His money's as good as anyone else's!" Said Wayne. "He's probably come to support his sister in her new business venture."

Croxley and his partner walked across the room to find seats, he sat down at Chloe's table; Jim left Dave on the door and went and sat with them. Chloe, who had seen Geoff and Wayne watching, looked across and shrugged her shoulders.

Abigail changed the CD, *Tubular Bells*, by Mike Oldfield, would play reasonably quietly in the background until the performers were ready to start at eight thirty.

Brian came out from behind the bar and walked over to Geoff and Wayne who were over by the mixing desk where Abigail was sat.

"What time are you kicking off Geoff?" he said.

"Any minute now," said Geoff "As soon as Chloe comes out of the ladies we're ready."

"Do you mind if I introduce you?" asked Brian "It'll give me a chance to plug the venue."

"No problem!" said Geoff "Look' Chloe's on her way back now, come on let's give it to them."

Elderflower Punch took to the stage. Geoff plugged his guitar lead into the jack-socket on the stage box, on the floor in front of him. "Nice company you're keeping." He said to Chloe as he helped her up on to the stage.

"Tell me about it," said Chloe sarcastically.

Wayne plugged into the Trace Elliot bass amplifier at the back of the stage. The three of them took their positions, Geoff on the right hand microphone, Wayne on the left and Chloe in the middle. Brian climbed on stage and moved in on Chloe's microphone. There was a rapturous applause.

"GIVE US A SONG BRIAN!" Shouted someone sat near the front; this was followed by shouts of "Yeah" and even more clapping.

Brian smiled at the audience, "There's enough talent here tonight to give you a song," he said, "I'm a retired performer who has now moved into the promotion business."

Brian spent the next couple of minutes welcoming the audience to the 'Opening Night at the Grey Mare' and told them his plans to make the pub the best music venue in the area and how all musical tastes would be catered for.

"You need to get a bigger car-park then!" shouted an irate member of the audience, "We've had to walk from halfway up Monkswood Lane".

This comment caused a titter in the audience.

Geoff looked at Brian and noticed that he was uncomfortable with this outburst, although Brian had absolutely no trouble shouting down hecklers and giving them 'as good as he got' he was a person who struggled to take criticism and someone was criticising his new venture.

Brian pointed to the culprit and said "Think of the weight you'll lose walking up that hill, do it two or three times and that T-shirt you've got on might actually start to fit."

The audience loved it, this was classic Brian Clayton Stuff; even the bloke who had made the complaint was in stitches.

Brian addressed the audience again, "We've got some great entertainment tonight ladies and gentleman, and please remember that all proceeds go towards Lute's benefit collection. So, without further ado I'll leave you with Elderflower Punch."

As Geoff played the opening chords, he scanned the audience and couldn't help noticing that Jim was in deep conversation with Stan Croxley.

The concert was superb, everyone performed well and at the end of the evening Geoff invited Woody and Pushing Forté onto the stage to finish off with one last song. He thanked everyone for coming and announced that, including donations already received, the total now stood at eight hundred and seventy four pounds.

This announcement produced another rapturous round of applause from the audience.

"Thanks very much," said Geoff "and don't forget that there's Folk Music here, at this marvellous venue, every Sunday, starting next week, please come and support us." He went on "Now what would you like to finish off?"

There where shouts for; *Wild Rover, Whiskey in the Jar* and *Black Velvet Band*, which really didn't surprise Geoff at all, he'd already discussed it with the others and they were going to perform all three anyway; as a medley, for the encore.

Before he announced his intentions, a lone voice at the back of the room called out, "Hey Geoff, how about singing that one that you played at The Cave last week, you know - The Rose Of The Ribble Valley?"

It went quiet for a few seconds then a ripple of clapping hands and shouts of yes rose to crescendo. Geoff knew that Elderflower Punch could do the song but he wasn't sure about how Steve, Carol and Woody would cope with a sudden alteration to the plan. He looked at them and they gave their nod of approval.

Geoff was back on the mic "OK then," he said, "this is for the gentleman at the back."

Before he could strike the first chord another voice shouted up, it was Stan Croxley who had made his way to the front. He was waving a fist full of notes in the air. "If you can persuade my brother-in-law to sing it, I'll make your total up to a thousand," he said.

Geoff was shocked by the offer from Croxley and didn't quite know how to handle it, after all Brian had specifically said that he didn't want to perform. He looked across at the, now closed bar, for a reaction from Brian, Tina didn't look very happy at all and Brian wasn't giving out any outward signs or indications of how he felt about the proposition. Geoff held out his hand towards the bar "That's up to Brian!" he said.

The audience went wild; most of them had very happy and nostalgic memories of going to watch Brian Clayton perform.

"BRIAN, BRIAN, BRIAN..." came the chant, it sounded more like a crowd at a football match than an audience at a folk concert.

Brian took the bait; he came out from behind the bar and made his way up onto the stage and stood behind Geoff's microphone, he picked up Geoff's guitar from its stand. "OK Just this once, for Lute" he said. He took the Capo off the neck of the instrument and put it in his pocket, he strummed the opening chord and started to sing The Rose of The Ribble Valley.

There was a loud rattling followed by a bang, at the back of the room; Tina had slammed down the roller shutters on the bar.

Chapter 22

Hook, line and sinker.

It was after midnight.

The crowd, now all gone, had had a wonderful night's entertainment, topped off with the unannounced return of Brian Clayton.

All the lights were on and Geoff and Wayne had stayed behind to help Abigail strip down her sound rig and load it into her van.

"She's gone Geoff!" said Brian as he came back into the concert room that was now completely devoid of any audience.

"Who's gone?" asked Geoff as he picked up his guitar case, ready to head for the exit.

"Tina's gone," said Brian "she's just fucked off and left me all because I sang that fucking song."

"She'll be back tomorrow when she's had time to sleep on it," said Geoff.

"She won't," said Brian, "I know she won't."

"Where will she have gone?" Asked Geoff. "Back to the cottage?"

"No!" Said Brian, "No-one knows where she's gone, she just walked out."

"Are you OK?" Asked Geoff, "Do you want me to stay?"

"No! I'll be fine," said Brian. "You've got enough to do without getting involved in my domestic problems, but thanks for the offer, it's much appreciated."

"I'll see you next Sunday then," said Geoff, "assuming that everything carrying on as planned?"

"It certainly is!" Brian replied, "I'm not letting the actions of some neurotic cow fuck-up my plans. Who knows, maybe I'll do a couple of songs myself."

"I doubt it," thought Geoff, he had been observing Brian, in his new role of Landlord, throughout the night. It was obvious that making money had become his new goal in life.

Geoff was somewhat disappointed that Brian hadn't donated anything to the evening's total, he hadn't even bought a drink for the singers and musicians who had given their services for free.

Geoff said his goodbyes and made his way out through the door; he heard Brian slide two or three heavy bolts into place. As he walked across to where his car was parked he couldn't help noticing that a Jaguar was parked over by the bowling greens; he could just about make out the registration number in the moonlight, it was T1 NAS.

Geoff thought it strange that if Tina had suddenly decided to do a runner, she would leave her car behind.

Abigail's Transit van was still on the small car park, as he got closer to it he jumped as the sudden noise of the engine trying to start gave him a shock. The window came down and Abigail's head popped out.

"It doesn't want to go!" She said, "Care to help a damsel in distress?"

"I'll have a look if you want," said Geoff, "Have you got a torch?"

"No said Abigail but why mess around in the dark, let's lock it up, spend a 'cosy' night together at your place and come back tomorrow, when it's light."

He couldn't believe what he was hearing. "I snore!" He said, with a smile "I might keep you awake."

"What I have in mind isn't exactly sleeping," she said as she stretched her hand out, through the open window, pulled him towards herself and planted what could only be described as a very passionate kiss, full onto his lips.

"There's plenty more were that came from." She said, smiling at him as she pulled her head away.

"I was very much hoping there would be." Said Geoff as he opened the van door and helped her out. This time she was willing to take his hand and let him play the gentleman.

Abigail was more than accommodating. When they arrived at Geoff's terraced house her first priority was to find the bedroom and get undressed and then climb in. Her only demand was that Geoff should bring his portable cassette player into the bedroom and play loud music while they performed. Geoff selected *Rumours,* by Fleetwood Mac and when he realised, that during the act of lovemaking, Abigail moved, in time with the music, he was delighted with his choice. Mick Fleetwood and Co. liked to do a fast number followed by a slow number and that made his first sexual experience with Abigail very interesting indeed. He found it difficult to believe that she stopped 'dead' when side one finished and made him get out of bed to turn the tape over.

He was completely spent about halfway through the side two, he put both arms around her, nestled up against her naked back and said that it was time to go to sleep.

"I'll make a mental note," said Abigail, with a giggle in her voice, "Folk Singers don't have any staying power."

"You really know how to pamper to a man's ego." He said and then drifted off into a deep sleep.

He woke up at ten o'clock; Abigail was still sleeping soundly. He got up to put on his towelling robe, the movement disturbed Abigail who turned her head and opened one eye.

"Good morning Folk Singer," she said with a smile, "Geoff wasn't it?"

He smiled at her, the world felt good, not only was this woman a terrific performer between the sheets, Abigail also had a fantastic sense of humour.

"You're wonderful!" He said.

"You're not too bad yourself!" She replied, "There's room for improvement but I've decide to award you eight out of ten"

"That good eh?" Said Geoff with a grin.

"Not too bad," she said with a smile, "My previous best was only a six."

"Tea or coffee?" Asked Geoff.

Tea with milk but no sugar," replied Abigail "And if you could manage to rustle up a couple of slices of toast I may re-assess and give you a nine."

Smiling to himself, Geoff went downstairs to the kitchen, switched on the kettle and put some bread in the toaster. He had assumed that he would be taking the tray upstairs and having breakfast in bed with Abigail so he was quite surprised, when he had finished in the kitchen, to find her fully dressed and sitting in the lounge.

"You're keen to get away!" Said Geoff.

"Not really," said Abigail, "It's just that I'm not a 'first thing in the morning person' and I really need to go and get the van and take all the stuff back to Uncle Charles." She went on; "I really enjoyed it last night Geoff, I don't mean just staying here, I mean the whole concert thing, it was brilliant. I've never really listened to folk music; I always thought it was about dead sailors and working class disasters. I didn't realise that it could be so entertaining."

"I like to think that it can be." Said Geoff, with a wry smile, quietly thinking to himself that it was a good job that Abigail's first experience of Folk music hadn't involved listening to some of the 'arty-farty' contemporary singer-songwriters who were doing the rounds.

"And of course the late night extras make it even more appealing. Maybe we could do it again sometime?" He said.

"I'd love to," said Abigail, "And I'm sure we will but I like to take things as they come, you know how it is? Without having to commit myself to any one particular relationship."

"I can live with that," said Geoff "But let's make it sooner rather than later."

"We'll have to see about that," said Abigail with a smile. "But now I really must get my van."

Chapter 23

A busy morning

"How did you get into the sound engineering business then?" Asked Geoff as he pulled out on to the main road. "You obviously know what you're doing when you're sat behind that mixing desk".

"I was taught by one of the best soundmen around." She said

"Oh yes!" Said Geoff "And who might that have been?"

"Uncle Charles!" replied Abigail.

Geoff smiled and said "Charlie Bagwell's never struck me as being a sound man, although he does like the sound of his own voice."

"Don't you believe it," she said, "Uncle Charles spent the late sixties and early seventies working full time doing the sound for chart bands, who were doing concerts in the big venues, in Preston, Blackburn, Bolton and Manchester. He really knows what he's talking about, you should ask him along to one of your gigs sometime, he would show you how to get the best out of your system."

"I'll bear that in mind." Said Geoff, quietly grinning to himself when he thought about what Wayne would have to say to that proposition. Wayne couldn't stand the sight of Charlie Bagwell.

They turned into Monkswood Lane and went down the hill towards The Grey Mare. It was raining heavily. Along the edges of the road there were several muddy makeshift lay byes. These had been carved out, over a period of time, by vehicles pulling over to let others pass. Several drivers had taken advantage of these spaces and parked their cars with two wheels off the road.

"Looks like one or two people decided to leave their cars and get a taxi home." Said Abigail.

"They probably got a taste for Brian's beer and decided to make a night of it." Said Geoff

"Or maybe they couldn't be bothered walking all the way back up the hill with a skin-full of ale inside them." Said Abigail, "The heckler was right though, The Grey Mare needs a bigger car-park." They reached the bottom of the hill and pulled up next to Abigail's van. Geoff got out. "Give me the keys and I'll try it," he said.

Abigail had got out, at the passenger door, and was walking over to the front of her van.

"You really must stop trying to be a knight in shining armour, it doesn't become you." Said Abigail. She ran her fingers along the slot at the top of the grill, flicked a catch and opened the bonnet.

"There!" She said, "It's always happening." She waved the dangling end of the HT lead in front of him and then pushed it back firmly into the connector on the end of the ignition coil.

She climbed into the driver's seat and turned the key, the engine came to life. She wound down the window. "These things are sent to try us." She said with a sarcastic smile.

"I suppose the lead jumped out by itself?" Said Geoff, playing along. He knew that the girl had set the whole thing up and his manly pride was smarting a bit.

"I hope you're not suggesting that it was a ploy on my part," said Abigail, with an air of innocence "What sort of girl do you think I am."

Geoff already knew the answer to that one and had to admit, to himself, that he liked Abigail and considering last night's experience, he figured that she could 'set him up' as often as she liked.

"I wouldn't dream of it," he said with a wide smile.

"See you again Folk Singer." She said.

"Don't I get your telephone number?" asked Geoff.

"No point I'm never there," she said with a wink. "But I will see you again, you're OK." She wound up the window and drove away.

"Easy come, easy go." Thought Geoff as he watched the van pull away and make it's way up the hill.

Geoff noticed that the Jag T1 NAS was still parked in the same place that it had been last night and he wondered whether or not Tina had returned (if in fact she had actually gone anywhere at all). He decided to knock on the door and have a word with Brian, after all he wasn't being 'nosy' he would simply be offering support in the capacity of a 'friend in need'. He tried the front door first; there was no reply. He walked round to the rear entrance and rang the bell. The rain had just stopped and as he took his finger off the bell push, the clouds gave way to bright sunshine and Geoff's gaze was drawn to the rainbow that suddenly appeared. The end of the rainbow seemed touch the surface of the furthest of the two bowling greens.

There was some movement over by the old bowling hut that was situated between the two greens. It was the two old codgers who tended the green, they were arguing with Brian. It was quite obvious what had started the heated discussion; the nearest green had been rendered useless by having four large holes dug in it, one at each corner. The mound of earth, by the hole on the furthest corner, had a spade stuck into it. It reminded Geoff of something that he was secretly trying to forget: The grave in his dream.

Geoff walked towards the three men; they were far too involved in the argument to notice him approaching. Their voices were raised.

"Mr Croxley assured us that the bowling greens wouldn't be disturbed." Said one of the men.

"I'm assuring you that you will still be able to bowl here," said Brian " and you'll still have the best green in the area, I need this space for car parking!"

"Good morning!" Said Geoff, rather loudly.

The arguing stopped.

"Hi Geoff!" Said Brian

Geoff couldn't help notice that Brian's Wellington boots and jeans where full of mud which suggested that it must have been Brian who had done the digging.

"Not exactly great gardening weather?" Said Geoff, with a smile.

"Don't you fucking start!" Said Brian sounding extremely stressed out. He turned back to the two bowlers; "Look I have a visitor so this will have to wait, OK!"

"We shall have to see what Mr Croxley has to say about this." Said one of the old men. They walked away unhappily, muttering loudly.

"What do you want?" asked Brian abruptly.

"I just ran Bagwell's niece back for her van, it wouldn't start last night, so I decided to call in and see how you were doing, after all you were a bit upset last night, with Tina walking out and all." Said Geoff.

"Well I'm not upset now," said Brian, "I'm ecstatic, I just hope that wherever she's gone she went with a one-way ticket cause as far as I'm concerned I'm fucking well rid."

Geoff thought that this was a good time to change the subject. "What's with all the digging then?"

"Well!" said Brian, "I was thinking about it after the concert last night. That miserable noisy bastard, who was shouting his gob off about the car parking, was right. This place needs a bigger car park. I phoned a mate of mine, who works on the roads and asked him if he could Tar-Mac one of the bowling greens. He said that as long as they were built on clay there wouldn't be a problem and that he could do it tomorrow. That's what I'm checking for. So if you don't mind I'd like to get on with it, I'll see you on Sunday."

Geoff could tell that Brian, for whatever reason, wanted to be left alone. "See you Sunday then" he said.

As he walked back, along the path by the bowling green, his nostrils were filled with the smell of roses. He looked back across the green at Brian, who was walking towards the mound with the spade in it. Geoff wondered why Brian had made that hole so much bigger than the other three. Then he had a terrible thought "Maybe Brian has...? No!" he put the thought to the back of his mind. "Surely Brian wouldn't be capable of anything like that."

Chapter 24

Back to the business in hand.

Geoff drove home; his mind played games all the way. There were still a couple of questions that needed to be answered. First of all where was Rosemary? And now what had happened to Tina? Geoff couldn't help thinking, to himself that maybe the answers to both questions lay under the surface of the Monkswood bowling greens.

After lunch he made a phone call.

"Hi Chloe how are you today?"

"Brilliant," she said, "What a superb night and we managed to raise a thousand pounds, I can't believe it."

"We certainly did," said Geoff "I've got a feeling that Folk Nights at the Grey Mare are going to be something to behold."

"Well I'm certainly coming down to support the first one." Said Chloe.

"I was hoping to see you before then." Said Geoff, "Now that the concert's out of the way I want to get to the bottom of this business with Rose & Bryan."

"Fancy a drink tonight then?" Asked Chloe.

"Sounds great to me." Said Geoff.

"I'll pick you up at about eight thirty then." She said.

It was eight thirty on the dot when Geoff heard Chloe pull up outside the end-terraced house. He was ready and waiting, Chloe was always prompt. He locked the front door behind him and got into the car.

"What's your fancy?" asked Chloe.

"That sounds like an offer I can't refuse." Said Geoff, giving a wicked smile.

"I mean where would you like to go?" She said in her best school maam voice.

"How about the Brown Cow? I've not seen Dougie since before our last gig there was cancelled and I should really go and thank him for sending a prize for Lute's raffle."

"The Brown Cow it is then." Said Chloe.

Ten minutes later they were at the Brown Cow. The pub was special to both of them, it was here that Elderflower Punch had done their first paid gig and it was where Chloe did her first gig with the band. Dougie, the landlord, thoroughly appreciated the fact that good quality live music dragged in the punters and he would often slip the band an extra ten or fifteen pounds on the nights when the pub had done exceptionally well on drinks sales.

"Hello strangers," said Dougie, as Chloe and Geoff walked in to the empty lounge bar. Without asking he picked up a barrel glass and started to fill it with hand pulled best bitter. "And what would madam like?" he asked as he placed the foaming pint on to the bar top in front of Geoff.

"An orange and lemonade please" said Chloe.

Geoff made a grab for the pint.

Dougie put his hand up, "Leave it there a minute, I'll top it up when it's settled." He went on, "Take a seat, I'll bring it across. Oh and they're on the house."

The pair sat down at a table in the corner that stood on the spot were the small makeshift stage used to be. "Looks like Dougie doesn't intend having any more live bands at The Brown Cow then." Said Geoff.

Dougie came across with the drinks and sat down with the two musicians. "Good health!" he said. "Here's to the death of live music at the Cow."

"It's not that bad surely?" said Geoff, "you can still have solos and duos on can't you?"

"Geoff you know how much I like my music and as far as I'm concerned live music means bands." Said Dougie, "I don't mind booking solos and duos, as you well know, you've done it on your own often enough, but I always wanted the Brown Cow to be a live music venue and that means live bands. The council is enforcing the licensing law, the brewery won't pay for a license and if I pay for it I won't have anything left to pay the musicians that I book. Another thing, I'm a tenant; I can't compete with the likes of Brian Clayton and his new venture at the Grey Mare. I don't hold it against him, good luck to him, he deserves it God knows he's filled this place often enough."

"What are you going to do then?" said Chloe. "I mean now that you've stopped having your music nights."

Well I'm fifty nine," said Dougie, " and Alice is fifty six, I think it's got to the stage were we take what bit of money we have and run. I can't afford to retire but I can always get a job working in someone else's pub."

"You're not serious?" Said Geoff.

I've never been more serious," said Dougie "I've handed my notice in to the brewery and we leave at the end of next month. Don't be surprised if you see a new weekend barman at The Grey Mare."

"You're thinking of going to work for Brian Clayton?" asked Chloe.

"More than thinking about it," said Dougie, "I've spoken to him he says he'll have a word with his accountant to see if he can afford to take me on as cellar-man and Alice as weekend cook."

The door opened and one of the local farmers walked in, he shouted out, jokingly, "Is there any buggar serving or what?"

Dougie stood up, "Hold your horses Joe!" he shouted, "I'm on my way." He winked at Chloe. "I'm really going to miss this place." He said, in a voice that the farmer could hear, "Especially the well mannered customers."

"Poor Dougie," said Chloe as the landlord went to serve the farmer.

One or two more people arrived in the bar and quite understandably Dougie became too busy with serving drinks to continue the conversation with Geoff and Chloe.

"Lucky Brian," said Geoff as an intriguing thought crossed his mind; "he's going to benefit in more ways than one."

"He wasn't too happy last night," said Chloe "When you and Wayne were packing the stuff away, he was having a right ding-dong with Tina. She was shouting about him singing that song and said if he preferred his bit on the side he could piss off and leave her to run the pub." She continued:

"You don't think she was referring to Rose as 'Brian's bit on the side' do you?"

"I knew that they'd had some sort of argument," said Geoff, "It must have been about one o'clock, just before we left, Brian was in a bit of a state, he told me that Tina had gone, she'd left him, he said it was because he'd sang the song."

"She must have been pretty pissed off if she went at that time of night." Said Chloe, "She probably went for a long drive, away from all the people in the pub, you know, to sort things out in her own mind. I bet she was back the following morning to kiss and make up."

"I'm pretty sure that they didn't kiss and make up said Geoff; Tina wasn't back the following morning and she certainly hadn't driven anywhere; her car's still parked outside the pub." Geoff went on to explain about how he had come to go back to the pub that very morning to get Abigail's equipment, he left out the bit about Abigail stopping the night at his place but Chloe soon figured it out. He told Chloe about the mysterious holes in the bowling green and how he had experienced the sweet smell of the roses again. "The thing is I'm convinced that the answer to this Rose of the Ribble Valley thing is buried beneath that bowling green, the problem is now that if we start digging I fear we may find another body."

"Surely you're not suggesting that Brian has murdered Tina?" said Chloe.

"I really don't know what to think," said Geoff, "I'm having another pint, what about you?"

Chapter 25

Complications.

Geoff stood at the bar waiting for Dougie to finish serving an elderly chap who was involved in a rather noisy game on the half size snooker table, in the vault. The farmer, who had been shouting the odds when he came in, was leaning on the bar next to Geoff.

"How come you've stopped playing here?" Said the farmer "It were grand when you lot were on, we could have a good sing-a-long and a good laugh."

Geoff wasn't really in the mood to go into long explanations, however he wasn't going to completely ignore someone who obviously appreciated his singing and playing.

"Times change and things move on," said Geoff. "All good things come to an end, sometimes through no fault of your own."

Dougie, who had seen Geoff waiting and was already pulling him a pint of best bitter, had been eavesdropping on the conversation. "Take no notice of old Joe," he said with a laugh, "He'd be in here at quarter to nine on the dot even if we had a group of performing sea lions providing the music."

"It's nice to be appreciated," said Geoff. He paid for the drinks, picked them up and went back to join Chloe at the table.

"Good health!" he said, as he passed her the orange and lemonade.

"Thanks!" said Chloe. When Geoff sat down she continued with the subject of Tina's untimely disappearance. "I'm sure that wherever Tina is she'll be fine."

"Becoming a bit of an expert on the modern day Croxleys as well as the ancestors are we?" said Geoff, rather cynically.

"And what's that supposed to mean?" said Chloe, detecting the slight caustic tone.

"You and Jim seemed to be getting on very well with Stan Croxley last night," he replied. "It all looked very cosy."

"I was going to tell you about that" said Chloe; "Jim's gone off on a bit of a tangent and it's partly your fault. He started talking to Stan Croxley at the concert last night and he's got this crazy idea into his head, he told me about it on the way home."

"Surprise me!" Said Geoff.

"Apparently Croxley phoned Jim on Friday and said that he needed to speak to him about 'the misunderstanding' in the woods." Said Chloe.

"Misunderstanding!" Said Geoff. "That's a bit of an understatement, he was out to hang us until he realised that we knew about the boxes."

"Stan Croxleys' words, not mine!" said Chloe, she went on; "Jim reckons that Stan's worried about what we are going to do with the information, he reckons that we've got Stan by the nuts."

"I'm not exactly sure what you mean but go on." Said Geoff.

"Think about it," said Chloe, "Stan thought he was in complete control the other day, all the cards were stacked in his favour, he'd caught us trespassing on his land and Jim and I were already the subject of a court order stating that we must not enter Croxleys Wood. We would have got a hefty fine and you would have probably got a caution."

"Yes!" Said Geoff, "I see what you mean, you've got to admit it, mentioning the collecting boxes was a stroke of genius; that twat Stan soon changed his tune when he knew that we knew that we were on to his little scheme."

"You just don't get it do you?" Said Chloe, with some frustration in her voice "As far as Stan's concerned, we are now a threat to his operation and now that he's stopped panicking and had time to think about it, he has two choices open to him."

"Go on!" Said Geoff, now intrigued.

"He either buys our silence or shuts us up permanently." Said Chloe, quietly.

Geoff pondered on this; he didn't actually say anything but there was a noticeable 'Gulp'.

Chloe continued, "We have to thank the fact that those two gorillas from Ribble Valley Security witnessed what went on, otherwise Stan may have taken some drastic action there and then."

"Surely the security guards know what's going on? They work for Croxley," said Geoff. "They must be on his side!"

"They're paid to look after the warehouse and the factory," said Chloe. "They won't know anything about Stan's interests on the side, they probably thought that we really were badger baiting and Stan will be happy to let them believe that. Paying your security guards two pounds ninety-five an hour doesn't exactly buy loyalty and undying allegiance."

"I'm beginning to see where you're coming from," said Geoff. "So what's Stan said, is he offering to buy our silence?"

"Kind of," said Chloe, "As I said, Stan told Jim that he was sorry for the misunderstanding but there had been evidence of people digging up badger set in the woods. He went on to say that if we needed a few soil or wood samples, all that we need to do is ask and he will arrange it for us."

"What about the boxes?" Asked Geoff.

"Ah well that's where we start to see what a scheming sort of person he is." Said Chloe. She went on, "Jim figured that Stan was waiting for him to ask about the boxes so he decided to play him at his own game and deliberately avoided bringing the subject up."

"So how did Stan react?" Asked Geoff.

"He fell for the ploy," said Chloe. "He brought the subject up alright, he'd obviously given his cover story a lot of thought so it would seem a waste not to use it."

"Go on!" Said Geoff.

"He casually slipped it into the conversation but it was quite obvious that he was lying, his body language gave it away." Said Chloe; "He said 'Oh and by the way, those boxes you found are Malaise Traps they are there to collect insects for an entomological group at Preston University who are doing a study of variation in insect populations in the broad-leaved woodlands in Lancashire." She went on, "Jim played up to him and said 'I figured it must have been something like that'."

"I sincerely hope that Jim went along with it and accepted the apology and let Stan think that he'd fallen for the insect story," said Geoff.

"Sort of, he just said 'Thanks Stan, I'll be in touch.'" Said Chloe. Then when I was running him home he came out with a wild but dangerous plan, I wasn't sure whether or not he was serious or whether it was just the drink talking, he had had one or two." She continued, "He said that the Croxley's had messed up his life and he deserved some recognition from them by way of a share of their fortune, after all Frank Croxley is his father. He's also threatening to hand the details of Stan's little 'Narcotics operation' over to the authorities unless he gets a share in the profits. And, because he assumes that Croxley's wife knows nothing about her husband's extra marital sexual exploits, he is also threatening to spill the beans about Frank and his mother unless he gets his way."

"I knew that he was a devious bastard the first time I clapped eyes on him," Geoff snarled, "It must be something inherent in the Croxley genes."

"I know that he's not very well off, how many students are?" said Chloe "but I never had him down as a blackmailer. I phoned him this morning to try and talk some sense into him but he seems determined to go through with it."

"Is he sure that Frank Croxley is his father?" Asked Geoff.

"It would appear so," said Chloe. "After Jim was born, his mother never worked again and the rent and all the bills were paid, monthly, by a third party."

"Croxley!" Said Geoff.

"Looks that way," said Chloe, "When Jim reached twenty-one, the money dried up and the poor woman drank herself to an early grave."

"If he's that desperate, for the money, he could just sell the story of Frank and his mother to one of the Sunday Papers, they would welcome a chance to dish some dirt on someone as rich and powerful as Croxley." said Geoff. "And that way he couldn't be accused of extortion."

"That's one of the things he intends to do if he doesn't get his way," said Chloe, "But he figures that the Croxley's should pay and not the papers, he's got this urge to hurt them, if not financially, then maybe their reputation. I'm worried about him Geoff, he could end up in prison or worse."

"From my limited experience of dealing with Croxleys," said Geoff, "I think I'd be looking at worse. Much worse!"

Chapter 26

A photo opportunity.

It was Monday morning and work beckoned, it was a glorious day weather-wise so Geoff decided that he would cycle the four and a half miles to the factory. He classed himself as a fair-weather cyclist and thoroughly enjoyed pedalling along the country lanes en-route to work.

The prospect of settling back into the normal work routine was certainly proving difficult after the previous weekend and the relative excitement of the very successful benefit concert at the Grey Mare. Normally he tried not to let 'matters musical' interfere with his day job but he couldn't help wondering about the direction in which the band were going. They were now a threesome and had proved, that although they missed Lute, they could manage perfectly well as a trio. However being a trio didn't solve the problem of gigs being cancelled because of the ridiculous 'Two in a bar' rule enforced by the Public Entertainment License requirements, which stated that no more than two performers were allowed.

Some of the landlords who had cancelled had asked Geoff, if he would consider doing the gigs solo or with Wayne. He could understand their frustration. The problem was giving him a lot to think about, he knew that he was quite capable of carrying a night on his own. It was even better with Wayne on bass, he then had someone to bounce the patter off and Wayne's musical ability thoroughly enhanced the sound, but playing as a band certainly gave him the most satisfaction from an artistic point of view. Maybe the solution would be to try two directions, go out as a duo in the pubs and keep the band for occasions where the license would allow it. That evening he phoned both Wayne & Chloe and asked them to meet up on Wednesday night to talk about the situation.

Wednesday morning Geoff was called into his manager's office; his first instinctive reaction was that he must have done something wrong and was going to be carpeted. After all he had been somewhat distracted by other events over the past few weeks.

Maria was the site manager's secretary; she was sat in an outer office up on the balcony where many of the company bigwigs were located.

"Hi Geoff!" said Maria, "He's expecting you, just knock and walk in."

The sign on the door said: -

P REDMOND B.Eng.Hons
SITE ENGINEERING MANAGER

Geoff had served his apprenticeship with Paul Redmond, the Site Manager, some years earlier. They were never exactly great friends but the two would always acknowledge one another with a nod when their paths crossed, which was less frequently these days. Paul had progressed up the management ladder, while Geoff had decided that he was more comfortable with a life on the shop floor.

Geoff tapped twice on the frosted glass window and walked into the office.

"Geoff! Nice to see you!" Said Redmond, who was accompanied by two suited gentlemen whom Geoff didn't know. "Pull up a seat."

"Cheers," said Geoff. He parked himself on a blue upholstered chair on the opposite side of the table to the three men.

"I didn't realise that you were into this sort of thing," said the manager as he threw down a copy of the previous nights Lancashire Evening Post open at page four.

Geoff smiled as he focused on a black and white photo of himself complete with guitar and Wayne and Chloe stood on either side. The small headline read: -

FOLKS RAISE A GRAND

FOR DOWNS SYNDROME BOY

"The music you mean?" said Geoff.

"No not the music! You've been a frustrated rock star as long as I've known you," said Paul Redmond. "I mean the fundraising."

"Have you got some sort of problem with it?" Asked Geoff, beginning to wonder what this was all about.

"Not at all!" Said Paul, "On the contrary, the company directors are keen to encourage employees to get involved with charities, especially where local children are involved. They want to push it on the basis that it will be good for morale, good for the local community and will also generate some publicity for fund-raising functions that our employees are involved in."

"Not to mention 'The company image'," said Geoff, rather cynically.

"Well yes, there is that too." Said Redmond, grinning as he tried to dismiss the comment as a joke.

Geoff noticed that one of the suited gentlemen was smiling at this. Geoff wondered if he was thinking along the same lines, that maybe the Aerospace Company had decided that helping charities at home outweighed the fact that they were selling high-tech weaponry to ruthless despots in the Far East. Maybe it cleared the corporate conscience somewhat. The debate was always a bone of contention with Geoff, his principles told him that he shouldn't be working there, his lifestyle and monthly outgoings at the bank dictated that he should. "So where do I come into this?" Asked Geoff.

"Well," said the manager, "I've got to provide some input into this initiative, so when I saw the story, in the Post, it seemed an ideal opportunity to get something into Air-Lines."

"I'm not with you," said Geoff, "What's Air-Lines?"

"It's the name of the new company bi-monthly magazine," said Paul, " and I'd like to introduce you to John Fishwick, the editor.

One of the suited men stood up and leaned across the table to shake hands with Geoff. "Pleased to meet you," said the editor, "this is Dave Thomas who does our photographs." He pointed to the other man, the one who had been smiling earlier. "I'd like to make this fund-raising concert the front-page story in the first edition of the new look magazine. So, if you're agreeable, I'll take some details for the story, and by all means fill me in on any up and coming concerts that you are doing, you may as well take the opportunity to plug them. Later on Dave would like to get a couple of shots of you, one at your workplace and one, if possible, with the other members of the band outside the pub where you held the benefit."

"When would you want to do the shots?" asked Geoff, looking across at Dave Thomas. The expensive Bronica camera that was hanging over his shoulder, on a leather strap, suggested that he was always ready to grasp a photo opportunity. "I could do the workplace one now," said Dave but I'm going to be pushed to do the Band shot, unless you can manage this afternoon?"

"I'm supposed to be working!" Said Geoff.

"No problem said Paul Redmond I'll sort all that out, if you can get your two colleagues bought in then take the rest of the day off, get Dave to pick them up, take them for lunch and let me have the receipt, Maria will refund you from petty cash." He went on, "And Dave, run a couple of films off I'm sure that Geoff could do with some professional publicity shots.

Geoff re-considered his principles; "Bollocks to them," he thought. "Why waste an afternoon stood at a work bench when he could be living it up a little." He spoke to the manager, "I need to make a couple of phone calls to Chloe and Wayne so that they can be ready when we go to pick them up then Dave can do the workplace photo before we get going. Oh, and I'll have to go home and change and pick up my guitar."

"Thanks," said Paul' "and to show just how much it's appreciated I'll have Maria make out a cheque for a hundred quid to add to your total."

Chapter 27

Ground to be covered.

Dave soon sorted out the first photos of Geoff at his place of work. He took a shot of Geoff drilling a hole in the underside of an aircraft wing. It was completely false and stage-managed but the photographer assured Geoff that it would turn out OK.

Geoff's work colleagues took delight in wolf whistling at Geoff and he humoured them by taking a bow at the end of the photo session.

Geoff had arranged for Dave to pick Chloe and Wayne up between half past twelve and one o'clock. He knew that it wouldn't be a problem as Chloe, being a student, did most of her studying at home and Wayne never did much during the day. Geoff decided that he would take advantage of the fact that his manager had offered to pay for lunch, to treat Chloe and Wayne to a meal that evening. After all they had already arranged a band meeting to discuss 'direction' so now the meeting was scheduled for seven-thirty at the Brown Cow with a table for three booked in advance. Hopefully Chloe would offer to drive.

Geoff asked Dave if he could put his bicycle in the boot of his car, it would save him having to come back for it later. Dave agreed and arranged to meet Geoff on the car park at eleven-fifteen so that he could run him home to pick up his guitar and get changed for the picture session.

They pulled out of the factory gate and turned right on to the main road, in less than a minute Dave had to slow right down because of a large articulated lorry that, for no apparent reason, was slowing to a stop in front of them. The large red rose, of the Ribble Valley Electrics logo was emblazoned on the back of the trailer. Dave indicated right and pulled slowly out intending to pass but found his way impeded by another Ribble Valley Electrics vehicle that was also stopped but going the opposite way. The two lorry drivers had their windows down and were conversing with one another with no regard to the fact that they were blocking the highway.

"Bloody Croxleys! They think they own the road," said Dave angrily as he pulled on the handbrake.

"Well they own pretty much everything else around here why not the road too." Said Geoff.

Dave pipped his horn to show his annoyance, a hand, held up in an apologetic like gesture, appeared from the cab of the lorry in front. Dave flashed his headlights in acknowledgement, there was loud cracking and hissing as the airbrakes on the two lorries were released and the vehicles began to move.

They arrived at Geoff's end-terraced house with time to spare; Geoff removed the bike from Dave's boot and locked it in the shed. He invited Dave in while he got ready.

"Wear dark trousers and take a couple of shirts, plain colours if you have them," said the photographer, "That way we can chop and change your image as the various backgrounds dictate."

"Would you like me to ring the other two and tell them to take a couple of changes of clothing as well?" asked Geoff.

"Good idea!" Said Dave, "Tell them to avoid anything with patterns on the fabrics."

"You really take this seriously, don't you?" said Geoff.

"It's my job, I'm a pro," said Dave, "I like every little detail to be correct, like I presume you do when you're working out an arrangement for a new song. Don't forget your company is footing my bill for this little project, if you were paying for my time and a couple of rolls-worth of shots, there wouldn't be much change out of two hundred and fifty quid. I've got to be professional."

Geoff let out a whistle as he placed four plain coloured shirts into a holdall.

They picked Wayne up first and Chloe fifteen minutes later. She had obviously told her mother about the photo-shoot, Mrs Walmsley was still attempting to brush Chloe's hair as she was getting into the car.

"Put your clothes into the boot otherwise they'll get creased." Said Chloe's mum.

"Mum I'm a big girl now, leave me alone, I'll be home for tea." She said, obviously embarrassed by her mothers actions.

The three men chuckled. It was difficult not to like Chloe's mum.

As they pulled away Dave suggested that they should get the shot for the company magazine first and once that was out of the way they could think about some publicity shots for the band.

"Think about what you want and I'll see what I can do for you." Said Dave.

"How do you mean?" Said Chloe.

"You know," said Dave, "backgrounds, poses concepts etcetera."

Geoff butted in "You're the pro mate, we're open to suggestions."

Dave turned into Monkswood Lane his brief, from the company manager, was to photograph the band outside The Grey Mare. Being such a hot sunny day, the sunroof and most of the windows were open; halfway down the hill the car was filled with the acrid, but not unpleasant smell of hot tar. When they got to the bottom of the hill they were surprised to find that access to the car park was blocked off by red and white plastic tape strewn between posts that had been placed across the entrance. There was a rough hand-painted sign that said: -

PEDESTRIAN ACCESS ONLY
NO UNAUTHORISED VEHICLES PAST THIS POINT

Dave reversed and parked at the side of the road. The four of them got out and walked down the sectioned off footpath to the pub. There where various bright yellow road-working vehicles operating, one laying down a compacted hardcore of limestone chippings, another spreading Tar-Mac on top and a couple of large rollers slowly crossing the black steaming expanse that had been the nearer of the two bowling greens.

"Jesus!" Exclaimed Wayne, "That heckler must have really got to Brian the other night, he's extending the car-park."

Chloe spoke up, "It was only three or four weeks ago that Croxley refused to let us dig there in case we spoiled the bowling green."

"Can you smell it?" Asked Geoff.

"You mean the tar?" Said Wayne.

"No as well as the tar," said Geoff.

"I can," said Chloe "I can smell roses it seems to be coming from over there, where that plume of vapour is rising from the ground."

"That's just about on the spot where Brian was digging," said Geoff, "I'm never going to find Rose now."

Chapter 28

A grim discovery.

Dave was puzzled by this strange conversation between the three musicians; he looked at Wayne who shrugged his shoulders as if to say that he didn't know what the other two were talking about.

"Just an archaeological problem," said Chloe, realising that the photographer was listening in. "I was involved in a dig here a few weeks ago."

Dave suggested that they walk over to the front of the pub where he could get a shot of them with the pub sign in the background and avoid any of the muck, dust and clutter, caused by the men working on the car park, getting in the picture. He certainly was a professional when he was behind the lens and had the shots 'in the bag' in no time at all.

I suggest that we go somewhere a bit quieter to do your publicity shots," said Dave, "any ideas?"

"I'm thinking about it." Said Chloe.

As they were walking back across the original car park a small black kitten appeared from nowhere, they stopped to avoid tripping over it. It took an instant liking to Wayne and started to squeeze itself up against his leg. Chloe couldn't resist it; she bent down and picked up the kitten then held it to her cheek.

"Poor thing," she said, "Are all these nasty workmen frightening you then?"

"Hold it there." It was Dave who spoke, he had the viewfinder up to his eye and the camera pointing at Chloe and her new furry friend." There was a loud click as the shutter on the camera operated, it startled the kitten which immediately squealed, jumped out of Chloe's hands and ran off towards the pub.

Chloe looked disappointed.

"Never mind," said Dave "I got a great shot."

Geoff recalled his thoughts in the manager's office, that morning "Never one to miss a photo opportunity."

Dave drove slowly up the steep hill on Monkswood Lane he had to give way to two lorries coming down they were loaded with more Tar-Mac and hardcore. "Well did anyone have any ideas for the publicity shots?" he asked again.

"Yes!" Said Chloe "I have, turn right."

The three men were intrigued

She continued "There's a Wine Merchant on the old Preston Docks. It's based in one of the old dockside buildings and sign-written on the big green sliding door it says something about fine wines and there is a picture of a bottle of wine being poured into a glass. It would make a great background for us with a name like 'Elderflower Punch'."

"Nice concept!" Said Dave "Unless anyone's got any better ideas?"

Geoff and Wayne remained silent.

"OK Chloe, we'll go for it."

They pulled on to the now disused Docklands; the site was undergoing some sort of urban renewal and was gradually being turned into a marina style leisure complex with many of the original dockside buildings being converted into luxury waterfront apartments.

The wine merchants was quite a way from the actual waterfront, it was situated in a cul-de-sac alongside a place that sold part worn tyres and a wholesale pet-food warehouse. The large double sliding doors on the loading bay were closed. On one of them, in letters three feet high it said: -

ARTHURS VINEYARD

Wayne burst out laughing when he read it out aloud; he needed to know was it actually owned by someone named Arthur or was it skit on 'Martha's Vineyard' the North American resort?

Painted on the other door, just as Chloe had described, was a large wine bottle emptying its contents into a glass, to the right of which said: -

FINE BRITISH WINES

"Perfect!" said Dave, "I'll go and square things up with whoever's in the office. He came out with two men and a teenage girl, "This is Mr Greenwood, the owner," said Dave.

The man walked over, to the three musicians, Wayne reached out to shake the out-stretched hand that was being offered.

"Arthur! I presume?" Said Wayne.

"Sidney actually," said the man "Arthur seemed a good idea at the time."

"It certainly was," said Geoff "It's definitely made Wayne's day."

They all laughed.

"I'd be delighted to let you have your picture taken against my doors," said the owner. "As long as you promise to send me a copy."

"I think we can manage that." Said Dave.

They spent about an hour posing with and without instruments. Quite a crowd gathered to watch the proceedings. Mr Greenwood brought out wine bottles of various shapes and sizes to use as props, he allowed Chloe to use his office as a changing room and provided coffee during a natural break that occurred when Dave had to change his film. Dave had two shots left on the second roll; he invited Sidney Greenwood and his two employees to appear on the photos, one with and one without the band, they were delighted.

Before they left they thanked the wine merchant for his assistance and hospitality, he said that it was a pleasure and gave them a bottle of wine each as a gift. Dave promised to send him some copies of the photographs.

They got back into Dave's car. "Who wants dropping where?" He asked.

"First me, then Wayne then Geoff," said Chloe, she went on, "I'll pick you both up for the meal tonight."

"Why don't you come for something to eat with us this evening? Said Geoff to the photographer. "You'd be more than welcome, we really appreciate what you're doing for us."

"I'd love to." Said Dave "But I'm away this weekend and there's lot's to do before I go, like developing your photos for a start. But thanks for asking."

The car pulled out of the cul-de-sac and onto the road that ran alongside the dock basin. There was some commotion over at the other end, about four hundred yards away. There were lots of flashing blue lights coming from two police cars, an ambulance and a fire tender that were parked on the water's edge surrounding a mobile crane that was lifting something out of the water.

Dave put his foot down "Pass me my camera bag please Chloe" he said, then, speaking to the three of them, "You don't mind do you? This may be a great photo opportunity."

"Feel free," said Geoff "You're in charge."

He parked about fifty yards away from the commotion, grabbed his camera and ran towards the action. The three musicians got out to see what was going on.

"We need to stay by the car," said Chloe, "Dave hasn't locked it."

"We can see everything from here." said Wayne.

Coming slowly out of the water, suspended on the taut cable beneath the crane's jib was a beige coloured Jaguar. The number plate on the front was swinging pendulum-like, held on by one screw. It read T1 NAS.

"Brian! What the hell have you done?" said Geoff out loud.

Chapter 29

Every picture tells a story.

Geoff had spent the last half-hour or so soaking in his tub and reflecting on what he and the others had witnessed down at the docks, in Preston, that afternoon. It was now six thirty, Chloe had arranged to pick him up at seven-fifteen, the table, for three, at the Brown Cow was booked for seven thirty.

Radio Lancashire was blurring out nice and loud thanks to the fact that he had actually got around to replacing the spent batteries. Geoff had intended listening to the midweek sports report but his mind had wandered to events elsewhere. The presenter announced "Here is Nicola White with the News Headlines at six thirty."

It always amused Geoff that this particular newsreader seemed to have problems caused by trying to use a 'High Brow' BBC voice. She couldn't quite cover up her broad Blackburn accent, which stood out, like a sore thumb when she used words like; bus, how or now.

Nicola White started to read the news: -

"Police frogmen are searching Preston docks after a car was recovered from the dock basin this afternoon. It is believed that the Jaguar, belonging to Tina Clayton, the wife of Folk Singer Brian Clayton and daughter of Local Businessman Frank Croxley, was driven into the dock during the early hours of this morning. Police are concerned for the welfare of Mr and Mrs Clayton. Anyone with any information is asked to contact their local police station.

This is Nicola White on The Voice Of The County."

"Jesus!" thought Geoff, "Has Brian topped himself?"

He thought about what he had just heard, it sounded as though maybe the police thought that they were both in the car. Maybe they didn't know that Tina had walked out on Brian a few days earlier.

He phoned the police; "Hello Police enquiries, can I take your name and number please?"

Geoff gave the information and asked to be put through to whoever was dealing with the Clayton enquiry. He was put through to a WPC Crawley. Geoff explained that he was a friend of Brian's and that he had seen him at the concert on Saturday. He told her that Brian had been upset about Tina leaving.

The WPC suggested that it may be a good idea to send someone round to interview him, she asked if he would be in all evening. Geoff explained that he had a prior engagement at the Brown Cow. The WPC asked if would be OK for one of her colleagues to 'pop in' to see him at the factory the following morning. He agreed and gave her Maria's extension number so that she could let him know when the police arrived.

Chloe arrived at seven fifteen on the dot, punctual as always. Geoff was just about ready, having been delayed due to his phone chat with WPC Crawley.

"Did you see the six o'clock news?" asked Chloe, as Geoff got into the back seat. "They think that Brian and Tina are both dead"

"It didn't say anything about anyone being dead," said Wayne, "It said that the police were concerned about Brian and Tina's welfare."

"I know," said Geoff, "I heard it on radio earlier on. I've spoken to the police they're sending someone to see me tomorrow."

"How come you spoke to the cops?" Asked Wayne. "Do you know something?"

"Only that Tina beggared off on Saturday night yet the Jaguar was still parked outside the pub Sunday morning." Said Geoff.

"You didn't tell them about Brian digging up the bowling green then?" Said Chloe.

"No! I didn't," said Geoff. "But maybe I will tomorrow."

"Are you sure that's a good idea?" said Chloe.

"I really don't know what to think," said Geoff, "Brian's been a mate for years, I know he can be a bit of rogue but I really don't think that he's capable of something like that."

Wayne was listening to the conversation; neither Geoff nor Chloe had previously mentioned the fact that Geoff knew about Tina's departure or what Brian was up to on the bowling green on Sunday morning; he 'put two and two together'.

"You two think Brian's topped his missus and buried her under the new car park." He said shocked. "That explains all the 'whispering' at The Grey mare this afternoon."

"I don't know what to think," said Geoff, "Sometimes things are not as they seem."

Chloe turned into the car park at The Brown Cow. The pub was open but there was a large brightly coloured sign that had been fixed over the door. It read: -

FRANCHISE OPPORTUNITY
SAMUEL BROWNS PUB MANAGEMENTSCHEME
ENQUIRE WITHIN

Geoff was glad of the opportunity to change the subject. "It looks like Dougie's serious about packing it all in then," he said, pointing at the sign above them.

"That'll be the end of a bloody good era," said Wayne as they walked through the door "fucking licenses

"Would you mind curbing your language young man? I run an orderly house here, have a bit of respect for your elders!" They turned, as one, and laughed in unison as they realised who was chastising Wayne for using some rather colourful language.

"Alice!" Exclaimed the bass player as he walked across and gave Dougie's wife a huge hug "Elders my arse, you don't look a day over twenty five, it's about time you blew that sugar daddy out and ran away with me." Wayne and the landlady had always got on famously.

Dougie was in stitches behind the bar, he winked at Chloe, "Chance would be a fine thing," he said as he put two pints of best bitter on the bar. "And what's your pleasure love?"

"I'll just have an orange juice and lemonade please." Said Chloe.

Geoff picked up the two pints. "Put all the drinks and the food on the same bill please Dougie and I'll settle up at the end, my boss is picking up the tab."

"No problem" Said Dougie, Alice please show these customers to an empty table."

That was a laugh; all the tables were empty; Geoff, Chloe and Wayne were the only customers in the pub.

Alice had really made an effort and had set a table for three complete with candles and a huge vase full of flowers on it. "This is like the last supper," she said, "I won't be making any more meals at The Brown Cow after this. Now what's your fancy?"

It was obvious that Alice and Dougie had made a special effort for the band who had played at the pub and packed it to the rafters so many times.

They ordered the meal and Dougie brought a second round of drinks to the table, along with two bottles of wine, one white and one red. "The wine's on the house," he said, "It's a thank you for services rendered."

He poured out three glasses, Wayne asked Alice and Dougie to join them in a glass; they did. Geoff proposed a toast.

"To Alice and Dougie, may they find success in whatever they choose to do in the future."

"Here, Here" said Chloe and Wayne in unison.

Alice wiped away a tear with a serviette and turned to walk out, embarrassed by the fact that she had shown her emotions.

Dougie echoed Wayne's earlier sentiment, "Fucking Licenses, " he said as he followed Alice into the Kitchen.

"Which nicely brings me around to one of the reasons why we're here," said Geoff. We need to decide what we're going to do as far as the band's concerned." He went on. "We're OK playing as a trio at private functions and at most Folk Clubs but as far as pubs are concerned, it's a problem. If they haven't got a public entertainment licence, then only two people are allowed to perform."

How many, of the pubs that we play have got a license? Asked Wayne.

"As far as I know, only the Grey Mare," said Geoff "and we don't know what's happening there now do we?" He went on: "We've got a few bookings in the diary at venues were the landlords are saying that they'll have to cancel unless we are prepared to do it as a duo."

Chloe interrupted, "Look, I know that most pubs can't have more than two performing at once and you already know what I think about singing in pokey little smoke filled bars. Its daft throwing money away, you two do the places that can't have the full band, I don't mind."

Wayne butted in, "But Chloe Elderflower Punch are a band, not a duo, I say bollocks to them."

"Wayne," said Chloe, I appreciate what you're saying but there's nothing we can do about it. Don't let the bastards grind you down. You have to perform, the people who come to watch you every time deserve it, use another name for the duo if you have to but don't give up and stop performing, you've got to do your bit to keep live music alive."

"Jesus!" said Geoff, to Chloe, "You're really passionate about this aren't you?"

"You'd better believe it!" said Chloe; "so as far as I'm concerned the matters closed."

"That's female efficiency for you!" said Wayne. "Ow!" He said as Chloe jokingly kicked his shin under the table.

Geoff Laughed, "well thank goodness that's settled, I expected a right row."

Alice came in with the starters and the small talk turned to Brian and Tina, Dougie and Alice were not aware of the news which gave them some cause for concern, not only because they were both considering working at The Grey Mare but also they both considered Brian a close friend.

Throughout the rest of the meal they reminisced about the good times that they had had at The Brown Cow and the laughs with Dougie and Alice. It was nine fifteen when Alice was clearing away the sweet dishes and Dougie was pulling another round. The door opened and in walked Joe the old farmer, 'on the dot' just like Dougie had said on Sunday. He was only customer to arrive since the meal had started.

As Dougie put the drinks down on the table there was a squeal of brakes on the shingle car park outside. "Eeh up!" Said Dougie, "Things are looking up, it sound like they're racing to get here."

The front door opened and in walked a familiar face.

"Dave!" said Geoff, "What are you doing here?"

The Photographer pulled a chair and put a large brown envelope down on the table.

"The pictures," he said, "I have to show you the pictures"

"You could have dropped them in at work," said Geoff, "We didn't need them desperately."

Dave was panting, "You don't understand, look." He took the top print out of the envelope and held it up to show them.

It was the shot of Chloe with the tiny black kitten up by her cheek "It's lovely!" said Chloe, then she realised why Dave was so exited.

In the background of the photograph there was semi-transparent image of a young woman holding a baby, "It's Rose" she said.

Above the woman's head, in the vapour that was rising upwards from the hot tar, the words "Help us" were clearly visible.

Chapter 30

Things that go bump in the night.

"Who's Rose" Asked Dave looking at Geoff "You mentioned 'Never finding her' this afternoon at the Grey mare and now Chloe seems to think it's the woman in the picture."

"It's a long story!" Said Geoff.

"I'm all ears," said Dave, "and now it's personal; this Rose, whoever she is, has turned up on one of my pictures."

Geoff started with the phone call from Brian and Chloe filled in bits here and there. Dave was fascinated and Wayne, who didn't know the whole story, was spellbound too. The only bit they left out was Jim's relationship with the Croxleys.

Geoff was just finishing off the story when there was a loud metallic 'clang'. The four of them jumped out of their skins and sat bolt upright. Dougie, with his hand on the bell rope noticed their reaction, "What's up with you lot, you look like you've just seen a ghost." He rang the bell again "Last orders at the bar," he shouted.

"Same again plus a pint for Dave." said Geoff.

Dave showed them the rest of the photos; they were superb, far beyond the band's expectations. He said that he had made copies for Air Lines and some for Sidney Greenwood, the wine merchant.

They thanked Dave for the photos, finished off their drinks and said goodnight and good luck to Dougie and Alice.

Chloe pulled off the car park and went to the right, Geoff spoke up, from the back seat "Wrong way! Don't forget you're dropping me off," thinking that she should have turned left.

"It's too late now" said Chloe "I can't turn round it's a dual carriageway. I'll take Wayne home first." She could have turned round at the next roundabout and saved herself about four miles but she headed in Wayne's direction and dropped him off at about twenty past eleven.

As she approached Geoff's end terraced house she grabbed the inside of Geoff's thigh. "Earlier, leaving the Cow, I turned right on purpose." She said whilst sliding her hand up to his crutch. "I don't know why but I just don't feel like sleeping on my own tonight and I was wondering if you would mind if I jumped in with you? I just want someone to hold me close and I'd like that someone to be you Geoff."

Geoff grabbed her hand and kissed it. "Chloe I can't think of anyone I'd rather spend the night with but what I can't be doing with is the 'cold shoulder' treatment the day after. I'd like to think that our relationship could develop into something more than a casual affair; at least I'd like to try. Deal?" He said.

"Deal!" she answered.

She parked the car and opened the boot. "I've got some overnight things in here," she said.

"You'll have me thinking you make a habit of this." He said with a smile.

"I may do with you." She said as she handed him her overnight bag

She reached back into the boot and produced the bottle of red wine that Sidney Greenwood had given her that afternoon. "I hope you've got a couple of glasses, I was saving this for just such a special occasion."

They went into the house. Geoff turned on the stereo and pressed play on the tape deck. The room was filled with the sound of Paul Simon and Art Garfunkel singing *Bridge Over Troubled Water*. He went into the kitchen and came back with his tin opener, which luckily had a corkscrew attachment, and two large whisky tumblers. "Sorry I don't have any wine glasses," he said as he screwed the spiral metal spike into the cork.

"Can we take these upstairs?" Asked Chloe. "She took him by the hand and led him upstairs for the second time. She put her bag down by the side of the bed and took something out of her jacket pocket and handed them to Geoff. They were the candles from the table at the Brown Cow. "I'm going to take a shower," she said, "find somewhere to put those and light them, then you can come and sponge me down."

Geoff didn't need telling twice.

He went downstairs for the matches and a couple of small saucers on which to burn the candles, while he was in the lounge he took the tape out of the stereo unit so that he could play it in the bedroom.

Back upstairs, he pressed the eject button on the portable tape player by his bedside. Fleetwod Mac's *Rumours* popped out and fell on the floor. He kicked it under the bed "Sorry Abigail" he thought to himself.

He got undressed, made his way to the bathroom and was excited by the blurred image of a naked Chloe that was visible through the frosted Perspex door of the shower cubicle. He slid the door back and stepped inside, closing the door behind him.

Chloe looked magnificent, her hair wet and her firm breasts partly obscured by the sweet smelling soapsuds. Geoff reached out and gently pulled her towards him hoping for a passionate embrace. She pushed him away, "Slowly," she said and handed him the soap and the sponge.

She turned around and backed into him pulling his arms around her, one hand to her breasts and the other to the inside of her thighs she arched her head back allowing him to kiss her neck while his fingers explored her body. She turned round to face him then gently spun him around and pressed her breasts into his back, she wrapped her arms around him and massaged his chest slowly working her way downwards until her frothy fingers were working on his hardening erection.

She stuck her tongue in his ear and whispered "Time for bed!" She turned off the shower, opened the door, grabbed a large bath towel and wrapped it around both of them. "We don't want to wet the sheets more than we have to." She said.

Geoff took her hand and led her back to the bedroom; the candles were burning just bright enough to reveal that the bedclothes had been pulled back and that there were two glasses of red wine on the bedside cabinet. Simon &

Garfunkel were providing the background music. They climbed into bed both so eager to fulfil their mutual desire for passion that the wine was forgotten.

Unlike their previous encounter, which, looking back, had been nothing more than just a lusty spontaneous encounter, this was pure ecstasy they took each other to levels of pleasure that they had never even imagined could exist before tonight. When they were both spent he nestled up to her back, put his arms around her and cupped her heaving breasts.

They both fell into deep, relaxed sleep.

"Geoff! Geoff!" There was a loud whispering in his ear. He woke up.

"Geoff there's someone downstairs" Chloe was digging her fingernails into his shoulder.

Bang, Bang, Bang, it sounded like someone pounding at the back door. Geoff climbed out of bed, pulled on a towelling robe and went downstairs. Someone was definitely rattling the back door. He picked up the ornamental poker from the hearth and walked across to the back door and with the poker held aloft in his right hand, ready to strike the unknown intruder, he opened the door with his left. He didn't need the poker, the man pushing on the other side of the door obviously wasn't expecting it to open so quickly and he fell inside, rolling along the kitchen floor. He looked up at Geoff and said "Sorry mate, have I got you out of bed?"

Geoff looked at him bewildered, "Brian! What the hell are you doing here?"

Chapter 31

Burning the midnight oil.

Brian held out his hand in a silent plea for assistance, Geoff grabbed it and helped pull him to his feet.

Brian was dishevelled, unshaven and filthy. Worse still he stank like a sewer. "I could murder a brew!" He said to Geoff.

Chloe had heard the voices and came down stairs to find out what was going on. She was wearing her panties and one of Geoff's T-shirts.

Brian smiled at her, "It certainly looks better on you that it does on him." He said.

Geoff spoke; "Brian go and have a shower while I make the tea, I'll get you some clean clothes."

"Throw the ones your wearing downstairs," said Chloe, "I'll put them in the washing machine."

"Sound like a good idea." said Brian. He went up to the bathroom.

"Where the hell's he been?" said Chloe as she bundled the stinking pile of damp clothes into the washing machine.

"He didn't say," said Geoff. "But I think we could safely hazard a guess at Preston Dock.

"You sort some clothes out and I'll make the tea and rustle up something for him to eat," said Chloe "He must be starving."

Geoff sorted out a pair of jeans, T-shirt, socks and underwear for his unexpected visitor and left them outside the bathroom door. Brian came downstairs looking clean and tidy but still showing the stubble of a couple of days without shaving. Geoff invited him to sit in the lounge and Chloe brought in a tray with tea and lots of hot buttered toast.

"Cheers," said Brian "I'm starving, I've walked here from Preston."

"That's over ten miles," said Geoff; "You must be knackered as well as starving."

Geoff and Chloe went upstairs to get dressed and left Brian alone with his food for a few minutes. When they came back down the toast had gone, Brian held up the empty mug. "I don't suppose there's another in the pot?" He said.

Chloe did the honours, she brought in three mugs of tea on a tray.

"You do know that half the policemen in Preston have been swimming around the docks looking for you and Tina?" Said Geoff.

"So they've found the Jag then?" Said Brian.

"They hoisted it out this afternoon we saw it, we just happened to be on the docks." Said Chloe.

"Was it a mess? Asked Brian.

"Well it was wet through!" Said Geoff sarcastically; he burst out laughing, "Of course it was a bloody mess. What happened?"

"I'm not one hundred per cent sure but I think I must have driven it in to the dock," said Brian.

"Why?" Said Geoff, "Did you do it to get back at Tina?"

"I really don't know, it was a nightmare Geoff," said Brian, "a nightmare that turned real."

"Do you want to tell us about it?" said Geoff.

Brian downed his mug of tea and gave them an account of what had happened.

"It was Tuesday afternoon, I had been on a bit of a downer, Tina walked out on Saturday and I hadn't heard from her and despite what I said to you, at the weekend, I was worried about her. I thought that maybe she had gone back to the cottage and would put in an appearance in a couple of days, after she had had time to cool off. I couldn't phone to check because BT still haven't sorted the phone lines out at The Grey Mare."

"The guys who are doing the car park arrived with all their equipment, one of them asked if I knew who owned the Jag, that was parked over by the bowling green? And if so could I ask them to move it, otherwise it would get splashes of tar on it. I had a spare key for it so I thought that I would take the opportunity to drive up to 'Dunstrummin' and make my peace with Tina."

"When I got to the cottage there was no sign of Tina so I went next door to ask Stan if he'd seen her; he hadn't. I didn't go into details I don't like that slimy twat knowing my business."

"I lit the fire to heat the water for a bath and then went through the pile of mail that had accumulated behind the door. Most of it was addressed to Tina and was still unopened which suggested that she had not been back to the cottage."

"I had a nice long bath and decided that there was no point in going back to the pub. I wasn't going to open up again until weekend, not just because of the car park but because the music nights are booked from weekend onwards and let's face it, the pub's so far off the beaten track no-one's going to come down unless there's something on. So I chose to put my feet up and relax."

"I got myself a four pack of Sammy Browns out of the fridge and turned on the TV but you know what it's like on a Tuesday, all soap operas and cookery programmes so I decided to have an early night. The fire was still smouldering in the hearth and I thought that I'd better rake over the coals before retiring. It was when I picked up the poker I thought to myself, 'Why not try one of Tina's special brews,' I thrust the poker into the embers and went for the jug and the jar. I put the usual scoop of petals into the beer and thrust in the poker, God it smelt good, it reminded me of happy times with Tina, I thought 'Fuck it!' and emptied the rest of the jar into the jug."

"I can't remember feeling so relaxed and at one with the world, I dreamt that I was with Tina but it wasn't the 'now' Tina, it was the 'then' Tina, the Tina that I had met many years ago, she was young again, happy, without a care in the world. We walked hand in hand along the riverbank, I had my guitar and I serenaded her with love songs, the sound of the mighty River Ribble gushing over rocks in the background providing an accompaniment to the guitar. I had sung almost every love song in my repertoire, there was only the one left to do - The Rose of the Ribble Valley."

"I strummed the opening chords and started to sing, Tina twirled and danced on the grassy bank, I was singing the song just for her and she was dancing just for me. She really was My Rose of the Ribble Valley."

"I sang the last verse, or what I thought was the last verse, you know the one, it finishes with the line 'And make her forever my bride,' but I couldn't stop, it was like some strange force came over me and compelled me to carry on strumming. I started to sing a verse that was new to me and suddenly it wasn't a love song anymore, it became a horror story. The grassy river bank turned into a vast expanse of steaming black Tar-Mac, a fist punched its way through, it was Rose she pushed herself out of a hole in the tar and ran over towards me shouting something about 'The minstrel is ours."

"Tina was terrified she held my hand tightly, Rose grabbed my other arm they both wanted me, I felt like the rope in a tug of war game. Tina was shouting 'He's mine, He's mine!' Rose was shouting 'He's ours!' I was being torn apart by two women. I shouted "I LOVE TINA!" at the top of my voice. Rose let go immediately. Tina and I recoiled backwards into the river. As soon as I hit the icy water, I woke up; I was in the Jaguar with water gushing in through the open windows and sinking fast. I managed to get out, through the window, and I surfaced by the dock wall and swam alongside it until I came to some steps."

"Was Tina in the car with you?" Asked Chloe,

"I really don't know," said Brian, "I was totally out of it, I don't recall getting into the car or driving it to Preston."

"You're going to have to let the Police know that you're OK," said Geoff, "It's been on the TV and radio news they're concerned for your welfare and for Tina's too. Why not ring them from here."

"Do me a favour mate," said Brian, "Can you ring them for me? I'm a bit confused."

Chapter 32.

The boys in blue.

It took about fifteen minutes for the police to arrive after Geoff had spoken to them on the phone. He had expected them to be pleased that Brian had turned up and that they could call off the search. What he hadn't expected was for three of them to turn up in two cars and for them to caution Brian and tell him that he was to be held on suspicion of 'abducting' Tina. From the questions the police asked Brian it was apparent that they were extremely concerned about Tina's whereabouts and safety and without so much as coming right out and saying it, they suspected that maybe Brian had murdered her. They did allow Brian to ring his solicitor before they took him away; unfortunately he only got an answering machine.

He was driven off in a patrol car accompanied by two plain-clothed policemen.

The third police officer, who was in uniform, reiterated the gravity of the situation. He said to Geoff "I know he's a friend of yours but we really are concerned about his wife's welfare, I'd like to ask you a few questions and really it would assist me if you'd agree to do it down at the local station."

"Is that where your two mates have taken Brian?" asked Geoff.

"No!" Said the officer. "He'll be at the nick in Preston, he'll be OK."

"I hope so," said Geoff "I kind of feel responsible for him ending up there." He spoke to Chloe. "Will you be OK if I go?"

"Yes!" said Chloe "Let's hope it all gets sorted out."

Geoff got into the police car and fastened up the seatbelt.

The police officer seemed a pleasant enough chap. "Hopefully this won't take too long," he said "You should be home in time for breakfast."

"I hope so," said Geoff, "I'm gagging for a brew."

"I'm sure I can sort something out down at the nick," said the friendly copper.

They arrived at the small police station as they pulled up the policeman said. "I won't be doing the interview, Preston are sending down one of the CID boys who have been assigned to the case. You've no problem with that have you?"

"I'm a big boy!" Said Geoff, as he followed the officer into the station.

"Can I have the key to the interview room please Sarge?" Said the officer to the Sergeant on the desk.

The Sergeant reached across and pulled the keys off a hook, on the wall and handed them over without taking his eyes off the newspaper that was open on the desk in front of him. "The bloke from Preston's just been on the radio, he's on his way." He said.

The friendly copper showed Geoff into the interview room, it wasn't up to much. The walls were brick with several coats of cream emulsion paint on them and the furnishings consisted of nothing more than a table and four chairs. There was a twin deck tape recorder on the table.

"Will this guy from Preston be recording the interview then? Asked Geoff..

"I very much doubt it, said the copper, you're not under caution or arrest, he'll probably just want you to sign a statement." He went on "Now while you're waiting, Tea or Coffee?"

"Tea, no sugar please." said Geoff.

The policeman was back in no time with two plastic cups full of something that was warm and wet, looked like tea but tasted nothing like tea. Geoff took a sip and screwed up his face in disgust. "Vending machine I assume?" he said.

"That obvious eh?" Said the copper. "Beggars can't be choosers."

There was a knock on the interview room door, it opened and in walked a man dressed not in uniform but in casual trousers, round necked sweater and a brown leather jacket.

"Not brought your guitar then?" said the new arrival

Geoff looked at him bewildered.

"I've seen you a couple of times at the Folk Club in Walton-le-Dale," said the man, "I sometimes play there myself on Singers Nights."

"Nice to meet a fellow musician." Said Geoff.

"D.C. Rawcliffe." Said the man introducing himself, though not offering a hand to shake. He handed Geoff a form. "Would you mind filling your name, address etc on the top of here?" He turned to the copper "Thanks constable you can leave us now."

He turned back to Geoff.

"Right! You know why we're here, let's start with tonight's events. How did Clayton come to be at your house?"

Geoff explained about Brian trying to force the door.

"Did he say whether or not Mrs Clayton was in the car with him when it went into the water?" Asked D.C Rawcliffe.

"Chloe asked him that, said Geoff, but he said that he was very confused and didn't actually remember getting into the car or driving it, he said he was having a nightmare and that he woke up when the cold water hit him."

The detective tapped his ballpoint pen on his teeth he was deep in thought. "Have you ever known Clayton to take drugs?"

"No!" said Geoff. He didn't want to tell the detective about the rose petals.

"OK!" Said Rawcliffe, "Let's go back a bit." He opened the ring binder that he had placed on the table. "You spoke to one of my colleagues on the phone yesterday, W.P.C. Crawley I believe?"

"That's right." Said Geoff.

"Her report states that you believe Clayton's wife disappeared on Saturday night, would you mind just going through it with me again?"

Geoff explained about Brian being upset because Tina had gone, he also mentioned that he thought that it was strange that her car was still parked outside the pub.

The detective picked up on this immediately "How long after the conversation with Clayton did you notice the parked car?" he asked.

"Half an hour, maybe three quarters," said Geoff "It was still there the following morning when I ran the sound-lady back for her van."

"What time was that?" Asked the detective.

"About ten o'clock." Said Geoff.

"Did you see Clayton?" asked Rawcliffe.

"Yes!" Said the musician.

"Was he his usual charming self," asked the detective. "Or did you notice any marked difference in his usual behaviour?"

"He was stressed out" said Geoff "But that was because he was arguing with the two old guys who look after the bowling greens."

"What was the argument about?" Asked Rawcliffe.

"Brian had dug some holes in the near bowling green, he said he was looking to see how far down he had to dig before hitting clay, if he found clay then it would be feasible to TarMac the area to use as a car park." Said Geoff. "The two old guys were giving him a hard time."

"Tell me how big the holes were!" Said the detective.

"Well," said Geoff, "He'd dug four, one in each corner of the bowling green, three of them were quite small, the one furthest from the pub was bigger."

"What do you mean by big and small," asked the detective.

Geoff pondered for a few moments, "I didn't actually look in the holes, but from the piles of earth next to them I would say a couple of buckets full for each of the three small holes and maybe a wheelbarrow or two for the big one."

"Would the biggest hole be large enough to take a woman's body?" Asked Rawcliffe in a voice cold and without emotion.

Geoff shivered, "Look you're not seriously suggesting that Brian's buried Tina on the bowling green?" He had wondered about that himself, but now he felt like he was 'squealing' on a friend.

"Just a 'yes' or 'no' would suffice!" Said the detective.

"Well yes, I suppose so." Said Geoff.

"I know that you feel awkward about this," said the detective, "What with Brian Clayton being a mate of yours but believe me we wouldn't have asked you here if it hadn't been absolutely necessary." He went on, "We are genuinely concerned about Tina's safety, as are her family; and let's be honest driving a twenty five thousand pound Jaguar XJ6 into the docks isn't exactly rational behaviour."

The mention of Tina's family made Geoff suddenly wonder if Stan was involved in all this. Had he found Brian totally out of it, after the rose petal concoction and driven the Jag to Preston and pushed it over the dockside? He kept the thought to himself.

Rawcliffe stood up, "Come on, I'll get the Desk Sergeant to get someone to run you home, you must be knackered. I'll also want you to be available this afternoon to try and point out exactly where you think the hole is." He opened the door and beckoned Geoff to follow.

The Desk Sergeant radioed for transport and while he was sat waiting Geoff could hear Rawcliffe on the phone to Preston; "Get the heavy gang down with their equipment I think that the body may be under the Tar-Mac on the car park at Claytons' pub."

Chapter 33

A long day ahead.

"Thanks!" Said Geoff, to the uniformed police officer for dropping him off. He unlocked the front door and went inside. It was seven-thirty just about the time that he would normally be setting off to work, there was no way he could go in today, he'd only had about an hours sleep. He gave his boss a ring and explained the situation.

"Can't be helped," said his boss "Sort it out when you get back."

Geoff went up to bed, Chloe was lying, naked and fast asleep on top of the covers. It had been a hot night in more ways than one. Geoff stripped down to his shorts and climbed in, pulling the sheet over himself and Chloe.

Although he tried not to waken her she sensed his presence and rolled sideways so as to lie with her breasts against his back and her knees tucked in at the back of his thighs. She licked his neck.

"I thought you were asleep." He said in a gentle voice.

"In that case I must be dreaming about you," she said.

"They think that Brian has murdered Tina," he said, "they're going to dig up the car park."

She whispered in his ear "Don't worry about it, just relax, I'll look after you." She slid her hand down his chest and stomach until she reached the waistband on his shorts, she inserted her thumb underneath the elastic and made an effort to remove them.

Geoff got the message and obliged by lying on his back and sliding off his shorts, in no time at all they were in the throes of passionate lovemaking. Exhausted though he was, through lack of sleep, Geoff couldn't remember feeling so good about a relationship.

He woke up at midday. Chloe had gone.

He showered, dressed and went downstairs to make breakfast. On the top of the kettle was a note from Chloe.

"Didn't wake you, thought that you needed your beauty sleep. I have to see Jim about some archaeology stuff Ring me tonight.
Chloe
And by the way, I love you XXX. "

Geoff smiled to himself and again felt good about the world until of course he remembered what was on the agenda for the afternoon.

He listened to the lunchtime news headlines on Radio Lancashire.

"Police have cordoned off the car park at The Grey Mare, the pub belonging to Brian and Tina Clayton. Mr Clayton has been picked up by the police and is now assisting them with their enquiries. A police spokesman said that they are still concerned for the welfare of Mrs Clayton.
This is Nicola White with the lunchtime news on the 'Voice of the County'."

He picked up the envelope containing the photographs from the coffee table and flipped through until he found the one with Chloe complete with kitten and ghostly apparition in the background. The apparition was on the exact spot where Brian had been digging.

The phone rang; it was DC Rawcliffe to say that someone would be round in the next half hour to take Geoff to The Grey Mare.

The patrol car pulled up at the bottom of Monkswood Lane. There was a crowd of twenty or so people stood on the Tar-Mac. Geoff had not expected to see Brian but there he was, handcuffed to a uniformed policeman. One of the men left the crowd and walked towards the vehicle, it was Rawcliffe. He opened the car door to let Geoff out.

"Thanks for coming" he said.

Geoff got out of the car. "How come Brian's here?" He asked.

"He's not denied digging the hole," said Rawcliffe, "Although he maintains he was checking for clay. So we got him to point out the spot and if you could point out the spot too that should give us a starting point for the dig. We've also got the two green keepers down here they've pointed out where they think the hole was, one of them is within two feet of Clayton's cross, the other was a mile out."

"I suppose the memory plays tricks," said Geoff, "Especially now that the areas covered with Tar-Mac.

"It certainly does," said the detective. "That's why we've had you do it one at a time, that way you won't be influenced by the others."

Another man who was wearing white paper overalls approached them. "Are you ready?" He said to Rawcliffe.

The Detective nodded, he said to Geoff "Take me to where you think the large hole was."

Geoff walked across the newly surfaced area and stopped about ten feet away from the corner furthest from the pub. He turned around to try and get his bearings relative to the bowling hut and one of the wrought iron benches that were used by spectators. He took three steps to his left, stopped and pointed to the ground. "Here as near as damn it!" he said.

The man with white overalls was viewing the whole thing through some sort of optical device that was mounted on top of a tripod, at the edge of the Tar-Mac square. There was another one on the adjacent side of the new car park. Geoff assumed that they would be using them to pinpoint the locations given by the witnesses for accurate comparison. Rawcliffe walked across to the man in white, who had given him a thumbs-up, looked at his clipboard and nodded. He then came back to Geoff "Bingo," he said, you, Clayton and one of the green keepers are all within a two foot circle, that's a good enough indication for us to dig without having to get any infra red detection equipment in." Then with a smile he said, "We like to save the tax payers' money."

The man in white was using an aerosol containing white paint to mark a cross on the surface of the tarmac. Other men started to erect a tent around the spot. Digging up a body called for discretion and the operation must be hidden from prying eyes and from the cameras of the media who were turning up in numbers.

Rawcliffe led the way back towards the small crowd that was gathered on the original car park at the front of the pub. It was quiet until the compressor that would supply the pneumatic power, to the digging tools, was started-up over by the tent. Geoff looked at Brian, "Sorry mate!" he said.

"Nothing to be sorry about Geoff." Said Brian. "I keep telling them but they won't listen, they'll find fuck-all there except a big stone slab."

The uniformed policeman pulled on the cuffs, as if to chastise Brian for speaking and led him to a car. They both got into the back seat.

"I sincerely hope he's right." Said Rawcliffe.

Chapter 34

Confusion

It only seemed like a matter of minutes before the compressor stopped, the only noise that could be heard now was the quiet gurgle of the River Ribble on the far side of the remaining bowling green. All eyes were on the tent as the two men who had been breaking through the Tar-Mac and the hard core came out bringing the pneumatic digger and hosepipe out with them. Two more men carrying small spades, forks and what looked like garden trowels went into the tent.

"What's going on now?" Asked Geoff, who had been watching the whole thing, from a distance, with Rawcliffe.

"The heavy gang have got through the top layer, it's down to our scene of crime forensic boys to do the rest of the digging." Said the detective.

Suddenly a large car drew onto the car park and it seemed to cause some agitation and a nervous reaction amongst the policemen and detectives who were there.

"Fuck me it's the Super!" Said Rawcliffe to one of his colleagues. "What the fuck does he want?"

"He'll have come down to make a press statement," said the other detective, "Granada have got their cameras here, you should know by now that he's got fucking superstar syndrome."

Geoff smiled to himself, not only because of the noticeable effect that the arrival of the senior police officer had had on his subordinates but what also amused him was the way that, whilst in discussion with each other, the policemen used four letter expletives in every sentence.

The Superintendent came over to Rawcliffe and spoke to him obviously trying to ignore Geoff.

"What's the state of play Jack?" asked the Superintendent.

Rawcliffe was practically standing to attention as he answered. "Well sir, the heavy gang have broken through the top layer and the forensic boys have started to sift through the soft stuff underneath."

"Anything to show?" asked the senior officer.

"Nothing yet sir." Said Rawcliffe.

Then, as if on cue, one of the white suited forensic men came out of the tent and walked over to Rawcliffe. He acknowledged the Superintendent but spoke to the detective. "I think you'd better come and look at this Jack."

Rawcliffe followed the forensics' man to the tent with the Superintendent close on his heels.

After what seemed like an age but in reality was about five minutes, the policemen and the forensics experts came out of the tent. The detective and the senior policeman were walking back toward the cordoned off area on the original car park. They seemed to be having a heated exchange of words.

"I don't care how certain you are Jack, I'm telling you Clayton couldn't move that slab by himself, that's an old grave you've got down there I'm not going to open it without taking some advice from an expert. I'm not going to be made to look an idiot on a Croxley case again, I had enough of that with the drugs in the woods farce."

Again Geoff smiled to himself and wondered if the Superintendent had been one of the Dog handlers who had gone into the woods to 'bust' the hippies during the protest at which Chloe, Jim and Tina had been involved some years earlier.

"Can we have a statement yet?" shouted a bloke who had an expensive looking camera hanging around his neck.

There was some discussion amongst Rawcliffe, the Superintendent and another couple of policemen. The impromptu meeting broke up and Rawcliffe approached the reporter who was stood with two of his contemporaries and the three-man news crew from Granada TV.

He made an announcement.

"Superintendent Cookson will make a statement in about fifteen minutes. Meanwhile thank you for your patience."

He returned to the group where one of the officers was busy scribbling in his notebook. Geoff figured that he must have been working on the Superintendent's announcement.

Another car pulled onto the car park, it was a Taxi from Burnley. A woman got out; she was wearing a full-length bright orange sari, a chiffon headscarf and sunglasses. The cameras focused on her as she walked over to the car in which Brian was cuffed to the uniformed policeman, the window was wound down.

" You bastard! What the hell have you done to my bowling green?" As she shouted, she took off the sunglasses - it was Tina.

Chapter 35

A quiet night in.

"I didn't realise that you were actually there watching it all unfold" Said Chloe.

Geoff had phoned her as requested in the note that she had left attached to his kettle.

"How did the police react when Tina showed up?" She asked.

"I've never seen as many chins hit the floor simultaneously," said Geoff. "The only people who were smiling were the reporters and the crew from Granada who got the whole thing on film"

"How did Brian react?" Said Chloe.

He just looked totally pissed off with the whole affair, if I were him I wouldn't be making any comments until after I'd seen my solicitor." Said Geoff.

"They've let him go then?"

"Well they couldn't really hold him on suspicion of murdering someone that's turned up at the supposed crime scene, alive and well."

"What about Tina then asked Chloe have they charged her with wasting police time or anything like that?"

"No!" said Geoff "She hadn't done anything wrong, apparently she'd booked herself in for a few days of reflection and meditation at place over near Burnley, it's some sort of eastern religious thing, run by a Maharishi."

"That sounds like Tina," said Chloe with a giggle

Geoff continued' "Someone had a radio playing and she heard about what was going on when she caught the end of the story on the news."

Chloe changed the subject slightly. "Talking of news, the good news for us is that the forensic guys have contacted the university to tell us that during the course of an investigation, they have stumbled upon what looks like an old grave. And that if we would like to have a look we've got until Sunday, to check it out, before the contractors come and make good the damage caused by the digging."

"Is that normal procedure?" Asked Geoff.

"Yes!" She said, "They do it for several reasons, first of all it's you scratch my back and I'll scratch yours. They get a copy of our report, which saves them a lot of time on their paperwork. They put a line under where they left off and make a note: -

Site investigation passed on to the Local History Department, Lancaster University. See their report - attached.

And secondly if we see anything suspicious during a dig then we let them know. Proffessor Thompson once found a gun on a site up in Carnforth, it was proved to be connected with a murder in Lancaster. "

"That's all very interesting Chloe," said Geoff, "but when do we get to see whether or not it's Rose in the grave?"

"I wondered when you'd get round to asking that," said Chloe; "how does tomorrow sound. The Professor is supervising the dig in the morning, I gave him a bit of background about why I was interested and he has invited me to join the team. We're meeting up, at the site at ten tomorrow morning."

"That sounds fine to me," said Geoff, "should I meet you down there?"

"Does this mean you're not taking me for drink tonight then?" teased Chloe.

The thing is," said Geoff "I'm absolutely knackered, I've only got a couple of hours sleep last night. I thought I'd have a bath followed by an early night."

"Sounds like a good Idea to me," said Chloe, "I'll be round at eight. Should I bring my rubber duck?"

"You're incorrigible!" Said Geoff.

"I know!" said Chloe.

"That's why I love you!" said Geoff.

"Can I have that bit again please?" Said Chloe.

"Later!" He said.

He put down the phone and turned on the TV to see if the afternoons event had made the six o'clock news that was due to start in under five minutes. He was fast asleep in the chair before it started.

He was woken sometime later by someone knocking at the door, he looked at his watch it was eight o'clock on the dot. He knew that it would be Chloe, she was always right on time.

"How's your day been?" he said to her as he opened the door to let her in.

"From the look of you I would say not quite as tiring as yours," said Chloe, "You look like you've just woken up."

"I have!" Said Geoff.

She put her arms around his neck and gave him peck on the lips.

"You're exhausted," she said, "Why not go and have that bath and while I make us some supper then we can have an early night, we've a busy day tomorrow."

"That sounds good to me," said the Folk Singer.

Naked they lay together each feeling secure in the others arms until sleep came upon them.

Chapter 36

A very unhappy ending.

"More toast?" asked Geoff, as he rose from the table to refill the teapot.

"Please," said Chloe "It's going to be a long day, we archaeologists don't like to rush things you know."

"I've noticed" said Geoff "With a grin as he poured the tea.

Chloe blushed "I could get used to being pampered like this," she said.

"How about I get you a key cut this weekend, you can move in and then you'll be permanently pampered." He said.

She looked slightly shocked, yet at the same time very happy. She stood up and embraced him. "Oh Geoff that's a wonderful idea, are you sure that's what you want to do?"

"I can't think of anyone I'd rather share my life with," said Geoff, "So I'm serious, if you're up for it we can start moving your things in this weekend."

"It's a deal." Said Chloe.

"Great!" Said Geoff, "I hope it won't cause any problems between you and your mum."

"She'll be delighted," said Chloe, "she likes you a lot too."

She looked at her watch and then at Geoff.

He smiled "Come on then!" He said.

"We'll go in my car," said Chloe, "I've some equipment in the boot which might come in handy during the dig."

Chloe had parked her car on the road in front of Geoff's house. When they walked out he noticed that the lady who lived across the road was watching them through a nick in the curtains, Geoff waved at her and the woman pulled the curtains together very quickly indeed.

Chloe realised what was going on and laughed" She'll have me down as one of those scarlet women who spends her nights with young single gentleman."

"Well she'll just have to get used to it won't she," said Geoff.

Chloe got into the driver's seat and reached across to release the catch on the passenger door. There was a large dog-eared leather briefcase on the passenger seat, it had one of fasteners missing and only one end of the carrying handle was attached.

"Put it in the back seat," said Chloe.

Geoff picked it up; it was very heavy. "What have you got in here?" He said "The Elgin Marbles?"

"I don't know; it's not mine." Said Chloe, "Jim left it in the car yesterday, he should show up some time today, will you remind me to let him have it back."

Geoff picked up the bag and lifted over to the back seat. It was a cumbersome task and as he was manoeuvring to get it over the headrest, on the back of the seat, some of the contents spilled out. They rattled and bounced as they hit the floor of the car.

"Acorns!" Said Chloe. "I wonder what he wants with a bag full of acorns?"

She released the parking brake and pulled away, it was a glorious sunny morning. The conversation focused on Chloe moving in at weekend and whether or not they would need to hire a van to transport Chloe's belongings.

The main road was quite busy, Chloe indicated right to pull into the outside lane in readiness for the right turn into Monkswood Lane. Geoff got excited.

"Turn around and go back." He said as she turned into the narrow side road.

"What's the problem?" Said Chloe. "Have you forgotten something?"

"No!" said Geoff, "You missed it! The gates to Croxley's Wood were open, there was a van inside; I think it was Jim's. There was something not quite right. Let's have another look, I'd like to know what's going on."

Chloe did a three-point turn and turned left back onto the main road. They passed the gates just as two huge Ribble Valley Electrics lorries were passing the other way and obscuring their view.

"Carry on to the roundabout," said Geoff, "turn round and pull up onto the verge."

The roundabout was just over a mile up the road, Chloe turned round and headed back towards the gates. She indicated left and pulled right on to the grass about twenty yards from the gates. They got out; Chloe locked the car and they approached the opening. It was Jim's van OK but it wasn't actually parked in the entrance. From the splintered wood around the locks on the gate and the damage to the front of the van, it looked as though the vehicle had been used to ram the gates.

They could hear voices coming from the direction of the glade.

"Come on!" said Geoff, "Let's see what all the noise is about."

Chloe handed him the car keys "Look after these," she said "I've nowhere to put them."

Geoff took the keys and placed them in his pocket, he screwed up his face and sniffed the air. "Can you smell petrol?" He asked.

"There's certainly a strong smell of something," said Chloe, "and it's certainly not the roses."

They came to the glade and were taken aback by what they saw and what happened next.

"Watch yourselves! He's fucking crazy!" Shouted Stan Croxley who was tied up, cruciform, to the log that they had been trying to move when the security guards caught them.

"Who's crazy?" Said Chloe.

She soon found out.

From behind them another voice spoke. "Chloe love you shouldn't have come. This is between me and the Croxleys."

They both turned around. It was Jim. He was pointing a double-barrelled, twelve bore shotgun at them.

Jim continued, "And you certainly shouldn't have brought your lover along, I don't know what I'm going to do with the both of you."

Geoff looked Jim straight in the eye. "I don't care what happens to that shit!" He said pointing at Stan, "But if you hurt Chloe I'll fucking kill you!"

"My my! We are brave today aren't we?" Said Jim.

Stan shouted again, "He's doused the whole area with petrol, he's going to burn down the trees and all of us too."

Geoff noticed at least three five-gallon drums at various places in the glade. The smell of the petrol completely obscured the smell of the roses, which were still blooming in abundance, all around them. He realised that the bracken in which he and Chloe were stood was soaked in the flammable liquid. He started to inch away hoping that Chloe would realise what he was trying to do.

"That's far enough," said Jim. "Stay where you are, you're exactly where I want you."

Geoff noticed that as well as the shotgun Jim was also holding a cigarette lighter.

"What the hell's going on here?" Came another voice from the opposite end of the glade. It was Tina. She ran over to Stan and made a grab for the rope.

"You don't want to do that! Shouted Jim; keeping the shotgun tucked in the crook of his right elbow he held up the lighter with his left hand and lit it. "It could cause a fire."

"Walk over towards Geoff and Chloe."

Stan shouted, "Do exactly what he says, he's fucking crazy."

"That's a fine thing to say about your brother." Said Jim.

"What the hell's he talking about?" Shouted Tina.

"Do you mean that good old Stan's never told you?" Said Jim. "He's been secretly having his way with you in these woods, away from prying eyes, for all these years and he's never told you about your younger brother?" He looked at Geoff and Chloe, there was an insane gleam in his eye. "You didn't know did you, these two dirty incestuous bastard's have been shagging each other, in this very glade, since they were at school together. He can't stand to think of her married to another man, in fact he's extremely jealous of anyone who shows her any sort of affection, that's why he tried to bump your mate Brian off the other night."

Tina shouted again. "What's he talking about Stan? What does he mean by a younger brother."

Stan started to speak.

"Shut it Croxley." Said Jim, He held up the lighter and lit it again.

Stan got the message and stayed quiet.

"I'm your brother," said Jim "I'm here because Frank Croxley raped my mother and now he doesn't want to take responsibility for his actions."

"Rape my arse!" shouted Stan. "Your mother set our father up and blackmailed him. She was nothing more than a Preston dockside whore, a five bob port in a storm to any pox ridden drunken sailor on shore leave."

Jim spun round and pointed the shotgun at Stan. He let off one barrel.

Croxley's face disappeared; Geoff presumed that it must have been Stans brains that trickled down the front of his chest.

Tina let out a scream.

Jim spun around and pointed the gun at her, "And now it's your turn you filthy Croxley bitch." he said.

Geoff couldn't control himself, it was a reflex action he dived and grabbed Tina to pull her out of harm's way; he heard the bang and the whistle of the shot as it flew above his head. His instincts told him to get up and take Jim out before he had time to re-load.

He was too late, Jim, had other plans, he had dropped the shotgun and was bending down with his finger on the flint-wheel of the cigarette lighter. There was a 'whoosh' as the whole of the glade seemed to burst into flames engulfing Jim who dissolved in a wave of intense flame. Another wall of flame was advancing towards Chloe, Geoff shouted but he was too late, it swept over her. She ran out of the inferno blazing from head to toe. Geoff and Tina both went to try and help her; Geoff patted her with his jacket as Tina rolled her over on the dry part of the undergrowth. They managed to extinguish her flaming clothing, however the heat from the blazing trees and undergrowth was so intense that they had to move quickly. Geoff picked her up and carried her back down the track towards the entrance; it was like escaping from Hell.

He put her down on the ground as gently as he could, she was shaking violently, all of her exposed skin was badly burnt and erupting into huge blisters that would form and burst almost immediately.

She managed to speak; "Looks like that's one problem out of the way," she said, "Down to a duo now."

"I love you!" Said Geoff.

"I, I," Before she could get it out her head fell back and she died.

Geoff never heard the approaching sirens.

Chapter 37

Reunited.

It was Saturday morning; Geoff woke up at about nine-thirty. His head was throbbing, due to the effects of the alcohol that he had consumed the night before and the stress brought about by the grief of losing Chloe. It felt like his brain had become detached and was bouncing about inside his skull. Yet he knew that there was something to be done. Hopefully a refreshing shower and two or three cups of strong tea would bring him round.

He took the galoubet that he had found under Bryan's log and put it into his guitar case. The remaining rose that had mysteriously appeared at Cromwell's Cave was still there, dried but well preserved. He put the guitar in the boot of the car and set off for The Grey Mare.

As he passed the gateway into Croxley's wood, he noticed that the blue and white striped plastic hazard tape, used by the police at scenes of crimes and accidents, was strewn across the entrance. The gates were still open and Jim's van was still there, now on the grass verge just outside the entrance. A smoky fog hung over the wood that was obviously still smouldering in places.

He turned down Monkswood Lane and drove slowly on to the original car park, there were a couple of other vehicles parked there, one of them was a white van that had 'Lancaster University - Archaeology Unit,' written on the side in black vinyl letters, three inches high.

"Good!" Thought Geoff. "That means they're still here." He parked his car and made his way across to the dig site.

The police tent that had been there on Thursday had gone. It had been replaced by a number of canvass windbreak-like screens, which now surrounded the hole.

A man, about the same age as Geoff, stood over two younger women who were carefully sifting through small piles of earth.

Geoff spoke to the man. "Excuse me I'm looking for Professor Thompson."

"Then look no further." Said the man. "You're speaking to him."

Geoff must have looked surprised.

"You were expecting someone older?" Said the archaeologist, with a grin.

"I suppose I was." Said Geoff.

"That poses an interesting question for you," said the archaeologist, "Are professors getting younger or are you getting older?"

Geoff smiled and offered his hand as he introduced himself to the friendly professor.

"Chloe's Folk Singer!" Said the professor. "I've been expecting you." He went on "Poor Chloe, it's such a waste, I was all for calling this dig off as a mark of respect but something inside told me that that's not what Chloe would have wished."

"I'm sure you're right," said Geoff, "I know that Chloe would have wanted to get to the bottom of this."

The archaeologist went on "As I said, I had a 'gut feeling' that you would come here so I haven't allowed anyone to lift the lid yet. I thought that you would like to be here."

He led Geoff into the area enclosed by the screens.

Professor Thompson's team had been busy; they had excavated an area about eighteen feet by ten feet. The hole was about two and a half feet deep from the surface of the Tar-Mac to the stone slab that covered the grave.

"If this is where your Rose of the Ribble Valley is buried, then she's not on her own." Said the Professor. "Look at these!" At the edges of the excavation there were parts of other stone slabs visible but not completely uncovered. "It's obviously an old grave yard, we'll not disturb it any more than we need to."

"What happens to whatever we find under the slab?" Asked Geoff.

"We have a look, take a few measurements, make some sketches, probably take a couple of photographs then we put the slab back and cover it up. We're students of history, not grave robbers. Though we will take that stuff back to the university." The professor pointed to a cloth on the ground, on it were a couple of small crucifixes and some small spheres about a quarter of an inch in diameter.

"What are they?" Asked Geoff.

"Rosary beads," said the Professor, "they probably belong to someone who was buried here. My guess is that friends or relatives would have placed them by the grave. They may have even belonged to Rose."

"I very much doubt it," said Geoff, "I don't imagine that anyone would have visited her grave.

Two young men appeared with a hand truck, on it was what looked like some scaffolding tube and some chains. They were obviously members of the team.

"The lifting tackle's arrived." Said the Professor. "We'll get out of their way."

He stepped out of the hole and on to the Tar-Mac, Geoff followed.

"Are you sure you're up for this?" he asked Geoff, "Sometimes we open these things and the contents, to say the least, are not very pleasant."

"I'll be OK!" Said Geoff.

"Ready when you are Professor." said one of the students who had been unfolding the block and tackle.

The lifting equipment took the form of a three-legged pyramid, two legs on one side of the slab and one leg on the other. Hanging from the apex was a hoist with a rather large hook on the end of a chain. Two robust looking nylon slings had been looped around the overhang at each end of the stone slab and attached to the hook. One of the students was winding a chain that controlled the lift; he was taking up the slack on the slings.

"OK Ross," said the Professor, "slowly one click at a time." The student pulled slowly on the winding chain, 'click, click, click…' After a dozen or so clicks the slab began to move. The gap couldn't have been more than half an inch then suddenly the air around them filled with the sweet smell of roses that was now so familiar to Geoff.

'Click, Click, Click.... ' Ross was still pulling on the winding chain; the slab had now been lifted a good six inches.

The Professor was getting quite excited. "Geoff you and the girls stay out of the hole until we've moved the slab safely out of the way." Then he spoke to the two lads, "Ryan help me push it over to the one side, Ross lower it when I give you the nod."

In no time at all the heavy stone slab was safely out of the way and back on *Terra firma*.

The Professor looked into the grave then turned to Geoff, "Well I suppose you'd better come and have a look."

Geoff stepped into the excavated trench and across to the hole. He looked into the hole and then looked up at the sky and took a deep breath. "It's Rose!" He said. "And her baby! The bastards must have murdered the child as well."

There were two bodies in the grave, one an adult female, the other one a tiny baby. Both were reasonably well preserved, the skin had turned dark brown and was of a leathery appearance. The adult was clothed but the child was naked. Around the neck of the adult was a pewter rose pendant attached to leather thong.

"What happens now?" Asked Geoff.

"Like I said a couple of photos and a few measurements then we put the lid back on and fill up the hole." Said the Professor. "Why? Did you want to say a few words or something?"

"There is something I'd like to do." Said Geoff. He looked at the four students. "Only it's kind of personal."

"Would you like us to leave you alone for a while?" Asked the Professor.

"I don't mind you staying." Geoff said to the Professor. "You can represent Chloe, I know she thought highly of you."

The Professor looked at the four students "Would you mind giving us some space?" He said.

They headed off towards the river.

"Excuse me for a minute," Geoff said to the Professor, "I need to get something from the car" He went to fetch his guitar.

He put the guitar case down on the Tar-Mac, opened it and took out the galoubet and the dried rose. "Do you mind if I put these in the grave?" He asked.

"Not at all." Said the Professor. "Is that the whistle that Chloe told me about?"

"Yes!" It's a galoubet, it belonged to Bryan of Clayton."

He placed the galoubet and the rose, in the grave, close to Rose's head.

He picked up his guitar, sat on the edge of the trench, overlooking the open grave and started to play and sing.

"She's my Rose of the Ribble Valley
And I love her like the roses in flower
A maiden so fair with a beauty so rare
She's the prettiest bloom in the bower
With a fragrance like a garden in Springtime
And eyes like the blue in the sky
She's my Rose of the Ribble Valley
If I ever should lose her I'll die"

He only sang the one chorus, he was pretty sure it was his imagination but Chloe was singing the harmony and the sweet trill of the galoubet was weaving in and out of the words.

He put down his guitar and looked at Professor Thompson, He couldn't hold it back any longer, he cried like a child.

The Professor put a comforting arm round his shoulder. "Get it out lad! let it go!"

Geoff wept and wept, "I could hear them all singing and playing," he said.

"I heard them too!" Said the Professor.

Epilogue

A short drive home.

There was a smell of rubber and a screeching of tyres on the tarmac as the unknown driver of the mysterious vehicle set off at a racing pace up Monkswood Lane.

"Who the hell was that?" said Abigail as Geoff climbed into the driver's seat.

"Just some smart arse who likes making a noise at the end of the evening" said Geoff. He started the engine. He pulled slowly off the Grey Mare car park and drove up the hill on Monkswood Lane, muttering profanities under his breath.

Abigail could see that he looked uncomfortable.

"Just what is the story with that song?" she asked.

"Who cares?" said Geoff as he turned left on to the Clitheroe road.

He glanced to his right; parts of the wall that had surrounded what once was Croxley's Wood were still standing. There were no trees, to speak of anymore, the area was now full of buildings, some of them were red brick, others were glass-fronted offices but most were concrete-grey coloured industrial units. The wall had been breached every seventy yards or so to facilitate a roadway. Above each one of the entrances was an illuminated sign that read: -

THE LOST MINSTREL BUSINESS PARK

Beneath the lettering were the numbers of the units that could be accessed by turning down that particular road.

Geoff's mind was wandering a bit, he imagined Rose, complete with babe in arms, and Bryan singing their favourite song in the fragrant woodland, Chloe was there, on backing vocals and Lute was accompanying them on his mandolin.

Abigail broke the silence some minutes later, "I care," she said "more than you think."

"I know you do," said Geoff, "it's just that it's a long story."

"I'm in no rush," said Abigail, "Why not tell me about it when we're both tucked up in bed?"

"That sounds OK to me," said Geoff "Come on we'll use the tradesmen's entrance."

He parked the car round the back of the terraced house and unlocked the back yard gate. The security light came on and revealed that most of the yard was taken up by dozens of plant-pots with small oak trees growing in them, most of them were discoloured with black circular blotches growing on the leaves.

"Careful not to kick over any of the pots!" said Geoff.

"What do you want all these for?" asked Abigail. "You've enough to plant a forest."

That's the idea said Geoff, with a grin. "They're part of my pension plan.

APPENDIX (I)

The Rose Of The Ribble Valley - Bryan O'Clayton *circa* **1714.**

She's my Rose of the Ribble Valley
And I love her like the roses in flower
A maiden so fair with a beauty so rare
She's the prettiest bloom in the bower
With a fragrance like a garden in Springtime
And eyes like the blue in the sky
She's my Rose of the Ribble Valley
If I ever should lose her I'll die

While travelling the highway to Preston
When I first set my eyes on that maid
It was on one fragrant Spring morning
I had stopped for to rest in a glade

With a smile that would melt snow in winter
And flaxen hair down to her waist
She sang like a lark in a meadow
I wanted to court her with haste

I am but a poor wand'ring minstrel
I can't give you silver or gold
But I give you this song that I'm singing
Forever to have and to hold.

She said "Pray sir for what do you take me?
To tease and to tempt me like this"
Then she smiled and she walked right up to me
And offered her hand for a kiss

I plighted my troth to this maiden
As I knelt on the ground by her side

I'll return to that glade in the summer
And I'll make her forever my bride

Of course no one knows how the mysterious 'sixth verse'
goes, but maybe it was something along the following lines.
(G.D.)

Dire news of my Rose now awaits me
My feelings are all but in vain
For she carried the seed of her brother
And I never can see her again.

APPENDIX (II)

MIKE HARDING INTERVIEWS DR KIM HOWELLS MP AND HAMISH BIRCHALL, ADVISER TO THE MUSICIANS' UNION, ON THE ISSUE OF PUBLIC ENTERTAINMENT LICENCES (P.E.Ls.)

Originally broadcast 17.07.02 - Radio 2

(Thanks to Mike and the team at Radio 2 for giving me permission to use it).

The folk session - "The life blood of our traditional music", as Mike Harding put it - may well be an endangered species. Musicians getting together in pubs and bars to play the night away have always been an essential part of our heritage. However, there's a law commonly called the 'Two in a bar' rule which makes it illegal for more than two musicians to play in public together unless the premises has a licence. Recently, certain local councils have been enforcing the letter of this law and we've heard stories of folk clubs that have been running for twenty years or more being shut down under this rule. The issue has become of subject of much debate in the folk and wider communities and around 150 MPs have now signed an Early Day Motion in the House of Commons to legislate for change. Even the minister responsible for licensing, Kim Howells, has called the rule 'outdated and pointless". Mike Harding speaks to Dr Howells about plans for the new legislation.

INTERVIEW WITH KIM HOWELLS, MP

MH: I'm joined in the London studio by Kim Howells, who's a minister in the Department of Culture, Media and Sport, and he's particularly responsible for licensing. Kim, I have to do this because we've had loads of emails in and letters from people ... let's clear the air first of all and set the record straight - Somerset folk singers are your idea of hell, did you actually say that?

KH: (laughs) It was what they call a throwaway statement at the despatch box! It was because one of the Somerset MPs stood up and asked me if I didn't agree with him that it was a disgrace that he couldn't listen to three folk singers as opposed to two and it was a kind of ... it was a throwaway remark, and afterwards I had a letter from some Dorset folk singers who said, "You're quite right, they are rubbish!" (laughter from Mike and Kim)

Let's turn back to the matter in hand. You've actually described the UK's licensing laws as archaic and at times wholly stupid. In one case there was a folk club that was shut down under the 'Two in a bar' rule and apparently six musicians were just tuning up at the same time before the session started and a council official who'd sneaked in to check up on the place thought that they were violating the law and closed the session down. Well, I've got to say whether it was jazz or whether it was folk music it wouldn't matter, because that's hardly protecting our traditions and our culture is it? That's more like Stalinist Russia.

No, it's madness and it worries me a lot, actually. I think the number of venues are shrinking, not growing. You know, It's a very curious thing because music is such a very important part, not only of cultural expression but it's economically very, very important. It earns us a lot of money in terms of foreign currency, foreign earnings and so on and the very idea that you start to shrink the number of venues, well, it doesn't make any sense at all, besides the fact that we ought to be making sure that young musicians have got places to play anyway.

One of the places I want to move from is one that's very important to me and to a lot of people up here ... I'll give you an example: In the Sheffield area, the South Yorkshire area each Christmas, groups of people, all the villagers in some of the pit villages and what have you, would meet in their local pub and sing carols. They sing these traditional carols to slightly different tunes. Now, they are, to all intents and purposes, those are illegal gatherings of people. Surely we can do something about that whereby people are not illegal in their own pubs, just singing for their own pleasure?

Well, I don't think it is illegal, actually, Mike, I'm not absolutely sure about this but I was very worried that inadvertently we would be indicting people who simply sang along or whatever and as you know, in Wales it happens all the time.

They have, they've shut down various sessions, they've been actually closed down by the local authority, they've sent people round and said, "You cannot sing in this bar, you've got to get out". What I want to ask you is, why should the government have such powers over the private individuals in a little boozer having a bit of a sing-song?

I think, first of all, Mike, obviously we're not arriving at a kind of fresh moment in history. What we've got at the moment is a crazy rule where you cannot have more than two musicians singing in a bar, playing in a bar, without an entertainment licence. And what we want to do is to have all of this covered by one new licence and it'll be for music or dancing or entertainment of any like kind which is presented publically for commercial purposes or for gain. So in other words, you'd be felt to be a proper person to have a licence to sell alcohol and at the same time you'd have a public entertainment licence. In a sense, we can't have it both ways. Either we're gonna loosen up on this and allow more than two musicians or singers or whatever to perform in a pub or we're not and if we're gonna do it we've then got to decide, are we gonna have this as a kind of licensed activity? - which we think we should have because that's where you take the public along with you because you can reassure them that there will be a degree of control, that they're not going to be blasted out of their front rooms every evening - or else you have a kind of ad-hoc situation where maybe the situation could get out of control and you know, I've recently been in pubs where there's just been one guy and a bank of amplifiers and it's been pure misery for the boozers, let alone for the people who live nearby.

Kim, if I can just go on to some questions we've had sent in from listeners, very quickly, because I do realise you've got to get off to the house and various other things ... Roger Gall has emailed us to say, and I quote, "When you introduce this new licensing system, if pubs don't have an entertainment licence, will sessions and singarounds be banned?"

Yes, I suppose they would be. The landlord would need to get an entertainments licence to cover himself or herself ...

But this is not for gain, is it, you were talking about ...

Oh, I see, I am sorry, I'm sorry, I thought that you meant it would be professional musicians being paid ...

No, just sessions and singarounds, people just playing for their own fun.

No, they certainly wouldn't and I'm very keen that we should make sure that that facility is there. There shouldn't be a problem. As long as money isn't changing hands, then there's no reason why they should have to have a licence.

Right. Well, Keith Acheson writes in from Hertford to say how much he enjoys his singaround, singing songs of soldiering and seafaring, parting and ploughing, love and drink - he writes here - "No money changes hands, we enjoy some wonderful evenings. Why does English law criminalise this very English and harmless pastime?" I think you've already answered that - it does at the moment but you hopefully will make sure that it doesn't in future, is that right, the way I read it?

Yes, absolutely, and can I also say that if a licensee, a landlord or landlady, can get an alcohol licence, they will get a Public Entertainment Licence for free, so it's not going to cost them any more, so it's not going to put off people making venues available.

Great. And this is on the White Paper and this is going to be in the Queen's Speech, is it, in the next session of Parliament?

Yes, very much hoping that it will be. You can never tell and no minister can ever say that it's going to be in the Queen's Speech (laughs) ... I'm keeping my fingers crossed.

INTERVIEW WITH HAMISH BIRCHALL

MH: Hamish Birchall advises The Musicians' Union on public licensing and he joins me now from a studio in Broadcasting House. Hamish, could you just explain very briefly the problem behind this 'Two in a bar' rule?

HB: Well, as you said in your introduction, if you have more than two musicians in a bar, you have to get a special licence, which is called a Public Entertainment Licence.

And how much does that cost?

It varies enormously. If you were in Central London it might be £2000 or more pounds per year, if you were in a rural area it might be as low as £150 a year but that's only part of the cost because when you apply for the licence it triggers a whole new set of safety inspections and the discretionary conditions which the local authority can apply have quite significant cost implications of their own, like for example the requirement to install new toilets if you have more than two musicians. There are other examples ... the implications can be so severe that the venue decides not to apply.

So how do you feel this is affecting folk music, in your experience as an adviser to the Musicians' Union?

Because folk sessions traditionally take place in pubs, and local authorities over the last few years - I would say perhaps five to ten years - have been increasing their surveillance of non-licensed sessions, a lot of local authorities probably turned a blind eye but the squeeze on local authority finances has meant that if they think they can increase a bit of revenue from the licence fee, they'll take enforcement action.

But why should they have a right to license us, this is what gets me, is this a sort of Stalinist state we're talking about - Big Brother - do we need looking after so much?

I couldn't agree with you more and the Musicians' Union position on reform has been for many years that we think there should be an inbuilt permission in licensing for this type of premises for live music because separate legislation which already deals with safety and noise, we believe, is adequate to address the issue. I think there is a mindset actually, in licensing departments, that looks at the letter of the law and not the spirit of the law, enforces the letter of the law without regard for the implications culturally and socially.

Hamish, the minister Kim Howell says he doesn't need persuading that this law is, as he says, stupid and archaic. What would you personally like to see it replaced with?

We would like to see an automatic permission for live music in bars and pubs in England and Wales, subject to certain parameters, in other words a presumption in favour of live music built into the law. Unfortunately, I think what is being proposed by the government is rather the opposite, a presumption against the live music unless it is specifically asked for by the applicant.

So in other words it should be more proactive, the very act of having licensed premises should license it automatically for live music, for the kind of things we're talking about.

Yes, that is a built-in recognition that a tradition exists and it needs to be cherished.

How much notice do you feel the government has been taking of the Musicians' Union?

I think, in recent months, much greater notice. Of course, the success of the Public Entertainment Licence Early Day Motion in the House of Commons put down by David Heath which I believe has over 150 MPs in support which puts it in the top fifty of over 1700 Early Day Motions, has perhaps led the government to realise that there may be more support out there for sensible reform than they had previously thought.

So if I understand rightly, what you're saying is if the government doesn't become proactive and give automatic rights for people to make music in a pub, if they say, "We expect you to apply for it", that automatically, in a way, makes illegal any kind of session in any pub of any size from the very small corner pub that I play in to the larger pub where the folk club is, they're automatically made illegal overnight?

Well, that's right, under the proposals as they stand, unless you had set out in your licence application - it's called an Operating Plan - concise details of the music you intend to provide, in the lifetime of the business, it'll be illegal unless the local authority has approved that first.

Thanks very much, Hamish Birchall, for talking to us tonight. That's Hamish Birchall, adviser to the Musicians' Union, especially on Licensing Law.

APPENDIX (III)

Just as in the days of Bryan of Clayton, folksingers still attack authority in song.

At the time of writing Roger Gall (an enthusiastic campaigner for the abolition of P.E.L.s.) wrote this little ditty. I laughed so much when I read it I just had to include it in the book. (Thanks to Roger for giving me permission to use it).

SING IT ELSEWHERE
Roger Gall © July 2002

Sing it here
Sing it there
For the sake of the landlord
Please sing it elsewhere

Important to us, is to be able to sing
And thought by many, to be very fine thing
But councils officials, who can count up to three
Are making outlaws of you and me

Sing it here etc

I bring you news of a terrible fact
Singing in pubs is a criminal act
At the moment you're safe if there's only two
But there's even worse news, in the Parliament due

Sing it here etc

The two in a bar rule is to be taken away
Now no one will be able to play
Folk songs from England or music from France
Without official permission sought well in advance

Sing it here etc

They say "you can't sing, public safety I'm afraid"
It would seem to be fine, if your not paid?
It is only the Minister that understands
How the pub is unsafe, when 'money changes hands'

Sing it here etc

And the lads can crowd in, watch their team on TV
Need no, permission or a safe capacity
Can shout all they wish and nothing is wrong
Only, needing permission to burst into song

Sing it here etc

Football supporters with money to burn
Can wake up the neighbours, with no apparent concern
But you and the 'missus', you'd better beware
When you quietly burst into 'Scarborough Fair'

Sing it here etc

I would like you all to write your MP
Its time that they listened to you and to me
I don't know about you but I think this a farce
To hear politicians speak out of their ...(dispatch box)

Sing it here
Sing it there
For the sake of the landlord
Please sing it elsewhere